HACKING
THE
MISSION

Peter McLennan

Acknowledgements

To those who provided feedback on drafts of this story: thanks! The generous souls include Diane McLennan, Ken McLennan, Charles Skoutariotis, Courtney Edwin-Nweze, Daniel Harper and Tim.

The cover image includes "Chainsaw.JPG" © kallerna (CC-BY-SA-3.0), "MSI Laptop computer.jpg" © Kristoferb at English Wikipedia (CC-BY-SA-3.0), and "Burnt bark on a Gum Tree.jpg" © Bidgee (CC-BY-SA-3.0).

Foreword

This story is a sequel to my previous novel, *Who Will Save the Planet?* While it isn't necessary to have read the earlier story for this one to make sense, some things may be clearer and more credible if you've done so. You can obtain *Who Will Save the Planet?* in hard copy and eBook form from many booksellers. A partial list is available at the book's website: http://writer.catplace.net/jason.shtml. Note that the eBook version is free!

Hacking the Mission touches on a few scientific, mathematical and computing concepts. You don't need to know anything about them to follow the story. However, if you're interested, you can find more information in the notes that appear at the end of this book. Whenever there is a relevant note, this will be indicated in the text with a small number, like this:[5]

Chapter 1

Logging In

Jason wrestled to control the car. He'd entered the corner going way too fast. The SUV's wheels slid on the dirt track, spraying out clouds of dust. Jason's heart pounded as he pulled the steering wheel to the left as hard as he dared.

Almost there. The young driver cracked half a smile. David, in the passenger's seat, sat rigidly with his fingers digging into the upholstery.

The terrified face of a woman suddenly appeared in front of them.

Crap!

Jason spun the steering wheel to the right and the SUV lurched sideways, throwing David hard against his door. The vehicle started to tip onto its side; Jason had visions of his beloved Predator becoming so much scrap metal. It teetered on two wheels for a while, then decided to live for another day and dropped back onto all four.

The boys glanced at each other's white faces, then jumped out of the car and sprinted back to where they'd seen the pedestrian. A pall of dust kicked up by Jason's hooning hung over the whole of Mr McKenzie's field.

'You didn't get her, did you?' asked David as he ran.

Jason, easily outpacing his heavily-built friend, shrugged his shoulders.

The woman was still lying on the ground. Five or six other people were standing around her, and two were kneeling at her side. The boys reached the group just as the lady was being helped to her feet.

A lanky man, who Jason vaguely recognised, turned to face the boys. 'Are you two alright?'

'Did we hit her?' asked Jason.

'No, she's fine.'

The lady was brushing dust off her suit, which was way too up-market for strolling through a disused paddock. It was too up-market for anything around the town of Sapphire Bay, really.

'I'm sorry,' Jason said. 'I didn't think anyone would be around.'

'It's my fault. I didn't look before coming through the gate. I should have known better, since your father said you'd be practicing here.'

Jason peered across to the house next door, hoping his dad hadn't witnessed the near-tragedy. It could still turn out to be a tragedy if he was forbidden from thrashing his Predator around Mr McKenzie's field, because then he'd have to wait until he could get his licence before he could use his beloved car. Fortunately, Mr Saunders wasn't visible.

Jason turned his attention to the motley bunch before him. A couple of them seemed familiar. Although the lady was nicely dressed, the others were pretty messy. Most were wearing jeans that were well past their use-by dates, but one chubby guy stood out in a Hawaiian shirt and orange board shorts that went halfway down his calves.

'You were looking for me?' Jason asked the lady. 'What did I do?'

'You stopped the Prime Minister from making global warming worse.'

'Hooray for Jason!' said the man in the orange boardies. 'Jason's our Parry Hotter!'

'Oh, so you're reporters.' Jason felt a sinking feeling in his stomach. He'd had more than enough hassles with reporters.

'No. My name's Gillian Bradley. We're a group of people who are concerned about the plan to allow logging in Sapphire State Forest. We'd like you to join us, because of your reputation.'

Jason looked down. He'd hoped the business with the Prime Minister was over and done with. Even though he got his way in the end, the episode was just too heavy. When the PM and a professor and your father and your friends and everyone else in town all tell you that you don't know what you're talking about and it's none of your business, you start to believe them.

And anyway, that wasn't about cutting down trees.

'I think I'd rather not,' said Jason.

'You'd be a great asset to our cause,' said Gillian. 'You could really help us to stop the thinning.'

'Thinning?'

' "Thinning" is what the loggers call it, instead of "cutting down".'

'There's more to it than that,' said the tall man. 'They're up to something. My computer keeps going to their home page, and I never told it to.'

Jason thought for a minute. It's probably a virus. I'll bet I could fix it.'

'It's a bigger problem than just Tom's computer,' said Gillian. 'Whatever they're doing, we need to stop it.'

Jason screwed up his face. 'What would I have to do?'

'Just come to meetings with us. Be seen with us. Maybe you could say a few words to reporters.'

'Come on, Jason,' said orange shorts, doing a little dance.

Jason shook his head slowly. But before he could come up with the words to politely decline, his thinking was interrupted by a prod in the side from David, who was nodding towards the man with the sick computer. Emma, who went to the same school as Jason, was peeping out from behind him. 'Go on, do it,' whispered David while administering another prod. 'Everyone knows you've got the hots for Emma.'

Jason stepped away from David. Why couldn't that guy take anything seriously?

Anyway, Emma seemed pretty much unreachable. She was always 'out of it' at school and just lurked around in the shadows. Just like himself, Jason realised. Maybe she was deep and intellectual, but there was no way to know.

A couple of the greenies had strolled over to Jason's car. One of them was inspecting the bodywork while the other was pushing on the hood, making the vehicle bounce on its suspension. Jason wanted to go over and keep a closer eye on them but figured he shouldn't just walk away from the lady he'd nearly flattened. Fortunately the pair didn't mess with the car for too long before ambling back to the main group.

'Is it okay?' asked Jason.

'Seems to be. Except for the pollution it belches out, of course.'

Six months ago, that comment would have made Jason feel guilty, but now he just shrugged his shoulders. 'The environment isn't any of my business any more.'

'It can be,' said Gillian. 'But I know you've been through a lot. You don't need to decide straight away.' She handed over a business card, and the group turned and started walking back to the gate. Jason fancied that Emma half-smiled at him as she left. Maybe if he could fix Tom's strange computer problem, she'd be impressed.

'What a bunch of weirdos,' said David. 'You'd fit right in. Gunna do it?'

Chapter 2

A Tabled Invitation

'You've now heard our case in favour of legalising euthanasia, and you've also heard the other team's case against it.' Jason looked down at his notes. As the final speaker in his debating team, one of his jobs was to undermine his opponents' arguments. He'd scribbled down copious points while they were speaking, even though they never said anything he hadn't thought of himself while preparing for the debate.

'They made a lot of interesting points. They could be right that a cure could be found, or that the patient could just get better. Those things really happen, so we can't just ignore them.'

Behind Jason's back, one of other members of his team cleared his throat raucously. It was obviously fake and Jason knew what it meant: he was supposed to be trashing the opposition, not agreeing with them.

He skimmed his notes again, looking for another issue to attack. 'Cost. Yes, as the speakers in the other team said, if euthanasia was made legal, then the government would have to cough up money to pay for it. They'd have to put taxes up. Actually, that's a good point. Lots of people are struggling at the moment, so we really wouldn't want higher taxes.'

That wasn't going to make his team-mates any happier. He could feel their glares drilling into the back of his skull.

Remembering he was supposed to make eye contact with the audience, Jason looked around the classroom. It was pretty empty, which wasn't surprising: not many students wanted to spend their lunch time listening to a debate.

Ms Gow, who ran the debating club, sat front row centre. She wasn't a pretty sight: there was too much of her, and her dress didn't cover enough of her seriously sun-weathered skin. She was clicking her pen over and over, as she usually did when she was unimpressed. And she was always unimpressed. Her eyes were fixed on Jason with a glare that could spotlight rabbits.

Jason quickly looked away to avoid getting his retinas burnt, and attempted to recover the situation by summing up his team's main points again. Judging by the reduced frequency of the pen clicks, Ms Gow seemed placated.

'So, to conclude, you can see it makes sense for euthanasia to be legalised. It's just cruel to keep people in pain when they don't need to be and don't want to be. And it would free up hospital beds so that we could treat other patients instead of keeping them waiting for ages like now.'

Jason looked to the back of the classroom in an attempt to seem confident. It wasn't a good plan: seeing Charles Saint Michael, aka Bull, in the audience made him totally lose his train of thought. What was *he* doing here? There's no way that thug would voluntarily turn up to anything that wasn't compulsory. Ms Gow must have put him on detention.

There was probably time for only a few more sentences. Jason knew he should hammer home his team's position, but that just didn't seem right. If he'd learnt anything from his battle with the PM, it was that things were never totally one-sided. It was dumb to pretend they were.

'But these things have to be balanced against what the other team said. When you think about that, it makes sense for euthanasia to be illegal. So, I don't know, I guess it's impossible to decide. Thank you.'

Jason sat down, red-faced. That wasn't going to go down well, but what else could he honestly say?

Fortunately, lunch time was nearly over so there wasn't much opportunity for Ms Gow and Jason's team-mates to hook into him. The English teacher ranted away in her husky voice and was supported by occasional jibes from the others. Not surprisingly, the other team was declared the winner.

Jason didn't bother to defend himself. He knew what they expected of him, and they knew that he knew, so it all seemed rather pointless. In addition, he was keen to get out of the room before Bull was set free, just in case Bull wanted to thump him for his role in wrecking his lunch time. Not that it was Jason's fault, but Bull would never let a technicality like that get in the way of an excuse to bash a geek.

As soon as the opportunity permitted, Jason scooped up his things and strode towards the door. Just as he was about to escape, someone behind him grabbed his arm. Jason's head dropped and he turned around slowly.

It wasn't Bull. It was the leader of the other debating team. 'Thanks, mate,' he said with a wink.

'Don't mention it,' muttered Jason. He shook himself free and departed.

•　　•　　•

Lunch time the next day was supposed to be spent helping David with maths, but Jason couldn't find his friend anywhere in the library. Even though David had asked for the session, he'd probably forgotten about it and was still kicking a football around.

Jason grabbed a table and waited. His head was still ringing with the crap they lectured at him after the debate. Why should everyone have to take sides all the time? Were you supposed to simply ignore half the issues and make your mind up—then tell everyone else what to think?

'So *this* is where the library is,' said David, plonking his mass down on the chair opposite Jason.

After they got out their stuff, Jason explained the basics of trigonometry then got David to try one of the exercises in the textbook. Jason jotted down the answer while David drew diagrams of triangles and scratched down a few equations.

Jason resisted the urge to help. He drummed his fingers quietly on the table. Its surface felt strangely rough under his fingertips; looking down, he saw that Bull had etched his nickname into the wood. Stupid Bull. He was typical of the idiots who thought they knew everything and had to ram their opinions down everyone else's throats.

'Okay, I give up,' said David. 'This trigger-monetary doesn't make any sense.'

'Trigonometry,' corrected Jason. He went over the principles again, then David resumed his attack on the problem.

Maybe this one-sided thinking was just a school thing. Maybe people in the real world were smarter and knew that some things were hard to decide. Jason wondered whether he should consider himself lucky that the PM and other people in Canberra had taught him not to jump to conclusions, even though that meant he didn't fit in with the simple people around him.

'There,' announced David. He looked over at Jason's notes and, seeing their answers were the same, clasped his hands over his head in triumph.

'Easy, isn't it?' Jason skimmed through the problems in the book to find another one to test David with. 'Try this one: "A surveyor finds that the top of a tree makes an angle of twenty degrees from the horizontal. If the tree is 100 metres away, how tall is the tree?".'

David briefly crossed his eyes, then started drawing a diagram.

Trees. Yes, those greenies were another example. They were just looking at their side of the argument. There was probably a good reason for chopping down the trees, but the greenies weren't interested in that. 'Why do they want to chop down the trees?' Jason murmured.

David looked up, confused. 'Eh? Where does it say that?'

'I was just thinking about those greenies.'

'Oh. Yeah, I don't get that thinning stuff at all.'

'Obviously.'

'You're just jealous 'cause you're so scrawny,' said David, returning to his diagram. After staring at it for a while, he scribbled it out and started drawing a new one.

Jason flipped idly through the pages of his textbook. 'I guess they'll make paper from the trees.'

'What? Oh, that.'

'Sorry, I'll shut up.'

David fiddled with his new diagram for a few minutes, then put down his pencil. 'I reckon the book's got this problem in the wrong section.'

'It's exactly the same as the one you just did.'

'No it isn't. That one didn't have a tree in it.'

'Ignore the tree. Just think of it as a line with a length.'

'Ohhh.'

Jason looked around the library. There were dozens of shelves of books. That was nothing new, of course, but it made a difference when you thought of them as ex-trees.

'Thirty-six metres,' said David.

'What? Oh. Yes.' Jason looked across at David's pad, but David obscured his working by placing an elbow on it.

Jason narrowed his eyes. 'You cheated!'

'Who, me?'

'You looked it up in the back of the book.'

'Well!' exclaimed David, crossing his arms in mock indignation. 'You just don't realise how smart I am.'

'Okay, if you're so smart, do this one....' After thinking for a moment, Jason folded a piece of paper in half along one diagonal, then slid it towards the middle of the table. 'There. Your sides are lined up with the edges of the paper, so that's forty-five degrees. If the corner of the paper is fifty centimetres away from you, how fat are you?'

'I'm not fat; it's muscle. Muscle from playing rugby.'

'Yeah, right. Anyway, I bet you can't work out the answer since it's not in the book.'

David started drawing yet another diagram, and Jason's mind returned to the forest. He'd done a few of the bushwalks there with his parents. There were kangaroos and various kinds of parrots, and specky views from the track up Mount Gore. Plus all those trees were busily absorbing carbon dioxide which helped to slow down global warming.

'And why are the loggers spreading computer viruses—if they really are,' Jason said out loud without meaning to.

'Eh? Oh, that greenie thing. I reckon you should suss them out 'cause of her.' David nodded his head at someone over Jason's shoulder.

Jason looked around and saw Emma standing at one of the library's computers. She had her back to the boys, so Jason looked longer. Emma was too tall for the computer desk and was hunched over, but then she was always looking down. Her long hair seemed too black to be real and blended into the black of her shirt, which would have blended into the black of her jeans had it not been interrupted by a silver-studded belt.

'I don't think she likes me,' said Jason.

'Course she does. Smart athletic guy like you, how could she not?'

'Skinny geeky guy, you mean.'

'Well, let's find out.' David placed cupped hands to his mouth. 'Psst! Emma!'

'Don't do that!' demanded Jason, pulling David's hands down.

But the damage had been done: Emma was on her way over. Jason pretended to read his maths book so he wouldn't have to make eye contact, then pushed it aside when he realised how nerdy that looked.

'So what were you doing hanging around with those greenies?' David asked Emma.

'I like the birds in the forest. And my dad says we need it for tourism.'

'Oh, so that Tom guy is your father? Jason was worried he was your boyfriend.'

Jason tried to kick David under the table but only managed to bang the toe of his shoe against a chair leg.

'Missed me,' said David. 'And I told you you weren't the only raging greenie in this school.'

'I was when I was fighting the Prime Minister and everyone else about global warming.'

'Nup,' said Emma, focusing on the table. 'I just, um, didn't tell you.'

'Oh.'

Nobody spoke, but David's glare demanded that Jason try a bit harder.

Jason inhaled deeply for courage. 'I could take a look at your Dad's computer, if you like.'

'No need. But, um, we're doing a protest march on Saturday.' Emma paused and flicked her hair away from her face. 'It'd be good if you'd come,' she added without looking up.

Jason couldn't help but think Emma had just invited the table to participate in a protest march. David's eyebrows were flailing wildly, which Jason assumed was supposed to convince him to do likewise.

'Next Saturday?' said Jason, frowning. 'I didn't know I'd have to decide so quickly.'

'It's got to be then,' said Emma. 'Dad says we've only got a few days before the government decides about letting them hack down the forest.'

David's eyebrows were still all over the place. Jason wondered how long he could keep it up before he got forehead cramp. Unfortunately, he didn't get to find out because the buzzer marking the end of the period sounded.

Then Emma played a dirty trick: she looked at Jason.

Those deep brown eyes were more than Jason could resist. 'I guess I could come.'

As he trudged off to class, Jason kicked himself for getting sucked in. This was exactly the sort of thing he swore he'd never do again. The forest did seem to be a good cause, but what was the other side of the story? Fixing Tom's computer would have been so much easier.

Chapter 3

March Ado About Nothing

Jason stood under the autumn-coloured leaves of a liquidambar in the park, shifting his weight from foot to foot. A couple of dozen protesters had gathered on the far side of the park. Jason recognised some of them from when he'd nearly run over Gillian with his Predator. The strange guy who'd been wearing the citrus shorts was impossible to miss: today's shorts were luminous yellow, making his red and green floral shirt seem tame by comparison. Several of the protesters had crudely-written placards, saying things like 'don't misTREEt our forest', 'leave our leaves alone' and 'log off'. Most of them were pretty cringe-worthy, although the last one appealed to Jason's computer instincts.

Jason looked at his watch. It was only a few minutes until the march was supposed to start. Emma still wasn't there, and neither was her father.

Jason's parents weren't there either, even though Jason's father had agreed they shouldn't allow logging in the forest because the forest was a tourist attraction and tourism was good for business. Despite that money-grabbing reason, Jason was relieved that he and his father were on the same side. They'd clashed heaps of times when Jason had been battling the PM about emission controls to reduce global warming. Mr Saunders hadn't wanted emission controls any more than the PM had.

Even though he wanted the logging stopped, Jason's father was adamant that he shouldn't have anything to do with the protest. He said it would be 'inappropriate' for a respected businessman to be seen with a bunch of rowdy yobbos. Jason had assured him it wasn't going to be like that, although he didn't really have any idea what it *was* going to be like. Hopefully just a nice quiet walk down Pacific Street.

David had wimped out too. Rugby training, or something. He'd reckoned his absence would be better for Jason, otherwise Jason would have faced too much competition for Emma.

'Um, Jason?' said a quiet voice behind him. He turned and saw Emma and Tom striding towards the protesters, so he tagged along with them.

Gillian was trying to herd the rabble into some sort of formation but the rabble obviously preferred chaos. The guy in the bad-taste clothes seemed to have appointed himself leader of the march. Jason was fascinated by his display of gestures; his arms never seemed to make it below his head.

'That's Sal,' said Emma. 'He's not from Sapphire Bay.'

Jason nodded. 'I'd have noticed him before if he was. I don't recognise most of these people.'

'A lot of them are from Sydney,' said Tom. 'They help out at protests like ours, wherever they are.'

Sal was waving wildly. 'Jason, come up to the front with me!'

Jason took a step back.

'Jason, you're our hero. You should be here!'

'He'll be okay with us,' said Tom.

Sal shrugged his shoulders and turned his attention elsewhere.

After a signal from Gillian, Sal waved his arms and the group shuffled off. Pacific Street had been closed to traffic, and barricades had been erected on either side. It seemed like overkill since there were hardly any spectators. Jason had imagined it would be like those huge parades on TV, but Sapphire Bay wasn't big enough to have crowds like that. Or maybe the locals just didn't care whether the forest got cut down.

Despite the small number of onlookers, the police didn't seem to be taking any chances. Jason counted six officers, which is more than he thought Sapphire Bay had. Even so, there weren't enough of them to patrol the whole length of Pacific Street so they trudged along beside the gaggle of marchers. In some stretches there were more police than spectators.

The disappointing turnout didn't seem to bother Sal. He waved his placard in the air and shouted slogans at the top of his voice, which occasionally broke into a squeak. From time to time he turned around and walked backwards, flailing his free arm to rev up the other marchers in a chant of 'trees forever, logging never'. That seemed a bit lame, and Jason kept his mouth shut.

Emma and Tom were totally into it, though. Jason had never seen Emma so full-on. 'Come on, Jason,' she urged between repetitions. Jason lip-synched along for a while, but was glad to be in the middle of the pack of protesters so he wasn't very visible to the onlookers.

'Why are you hiding?' asked Emma. 'You should be proud! You beat the PM, remember?'

'It wasn't fun, though.'

'But it was worth it, wasn't it?'

Jason thought for a while, then answered 'yes.' While that was a pleasing realisation, he still didn't want to be the centre of attention. Or even the edge of it.

Fortunately, Sal was putting on such a good show that the onlookers didn't pay much attention to anyone else. They seemed more interested in watching the spectacle than showing any support for the cause. The only time they cheered was when Sal, walking backwards, tripped in a pot-hole and accidentally did a backwards roll.

The march took longer than Jason expected because everyone was dawdling. Sal's antics didn't help, either. By the time the council offices finally came into view, the heat rising off the road was making Jason sweat even though summer had finished a couple of weeks ago.

There were more spectators here. Most of them sheltered in the shade of the orange-leaved trees dotted around the council park. There was even a couple of TV cameras, one of which was pointing directly at the marchers. Jason manoeuvred himself so that Tom was between him and the camera.

Tom tapped Jason on the shoulder and pointed at a well-dressed man standing behind one of the barricades.

'See that bloke?' he said, nearly having to yell to make himself heard over the chanting. 'He's the enemy.'

'Who is it?'

'Boss of the loggers. His name's Wherrett.'

Mr Wherrett didn't look like a logger. Loggers didn't wear light grey suits or have upwards-combed blond hair. He looked much more like the sort of person who'd deliberately spread computer viruses. The man stood expressionless, just watching the rabble pass noisily by.

But the man beside him definitely looked like a logger. He was built like a gorilla, with legs as thick as tree trunks. He stared furiously at Sal but Sal was too busy conducting the procession to notice.

However, Sal noticed when the logger fired up his chainsaw and started hacking into a log. The raucous sound cut through the greenies' chants and a shower of wood chips blasted into the spectators nearby. The men with the TV cameras pushed in front of everyone else to get an unobstructed view of the action.

Most of the marchers edged towards the other side of the road. Jason was happy to do likewise. Emma grabbed her father's hand, which made Jason feel a bit jealous. Even though there were lots of adults around, and even police, Jason would still have felt safer if David had been there. David wouldn't have been worried about a loony with a chainsaw.

One of the greenies wasn't worried either. The short but strong-looking man positioned himself between Sal and the chainsaw-wielder and returned the logger's stare. The cameramen moved around so they could get the muscleman in the picture.

'That'll do, Einstein,' Gillian shouted, but there was no way the greenie could have heard her over the buzz of the chainsaw.

Two cops rushed over and alternated frantically between pointing at the saw and making cut-throat gestures. After a nod from Mr Wherrett, the burly logger turned off his saw and held it high above his bald head.

Einstein inched closer to the barricade in front of the logger while making a variety of gestures with his fingers and fists. Jason hoped the police could stop a fight breaking out: Einstein might have been muscly but he was at least a ruler-length shorter than the other guy.

Fortunately, Gillian and Tom rushed over and pulled Einstein back into the main body of marchers. The group sped up to get past the loggers and Sal resumed his cheerleading, though he was less flamboyant than before and glanced back at the chainsaw man from time to time.

Jason stole a backwards glance too. The chainsaw was still being held high above the logger's sweaty scalp. Jason wondered if there was any chance his father wouldn't find out about this. It was exactly the sort of thing he'd warned about. Einstein was now gesticulating rudely at the crowd for no apparent reason, and Sal was just plain embarrassing. Jason contemplated ducking under one of the barricades and disappearing, but figured that would probably draw more attention than trudging on with the mob. Plus, there was Emma.

The marchers finally halted in front of the council offices. Tom immediately broke from the pack and ran over to a yellow van, returning promptly with a PA system. After plugging a few things in, he handed Gillian a microphone.

'Ladies and gentlemen, thank you for—' The PA system was silent. Gillian looked at Tom, who fiddled with something and then gave a thumbs-up.

'Ladies and—' Feedback squeal. Gillian looked at Tom again, who shrugged his shoulders. Gillian tapped on the microphone but that made it worse. Jason could see some of the spectators sniggering. What a nuisance. He didn't want to move from his nice anonymous position in the middle of the greenies, but he couldn't stand to see Gillian embarrassed. He ran over to the PA system's speaker and repositioned it so it was in front of the microphone. The screech dried up and Jason skulked back into the mob. Gillian was too preoccupied to acknowledge his contribution but Emma smiled and nodded, which was much more valuable.

Gillian commenced once more. This time the PA system functioned properly—but after listening to Gillian for a while, Jason started to wonder whether that was a good thing. Her speech meandered all over the place, mentioning heaps of reasons why logging shouldn't be allowed but never explaining or justifying anything. If she'd been a member of Jason's debating team, Ms Gow would have ripped her to shreds.

Jason tried to look interested even though he wasn't. Many of the spectators obviously felt the same way and wandered off. Maybe Gillian should have let Sal do the talking; at least he would have been entertaining. Even the feedback squeal had provided greater entertainment.

The people who did hang around for Gillian's talk weren't exactly supportive. Most looked on silently with stern expressions on their faces, but a few of them punctuated Gillian's efforts with calls of 'says you', 'prove it', 'where's your evidence?', and the old classic, 'bullshit'. 'I'll bet they're loggers,' murmured Emma.

Gillian was getting flustered. She kept losing track of where she was up to and had to refer to her notes. She started saying 'um' and 'ah'. She looked over at the police whenever anyone shouted over the top of her, but the police just looked back.

Einstein strolled over to the loudest of the loudmouths and stood in front of the barricade that separated them, but the stream of criticism continued. The reporters that were filming Gillian abandoned their positions and scuttled over to the stand-off. Two policemen also hurried over and stood between Einstein and the barricade.

Gillian's speech seemed to go on for longer than the march. After she finally shut up, Sal attempted to whip the protesters up into another frenzy of chanting, but he only got a half-hearted response.

After a few minutes of forced noise, Gillian tapped on her watch and the protesters fell silent. Workmen started collecting up the barricades and the few remaining spectators drifted away. Jason watched with relief as Mr Wherrett and the chainsaw man got into a dirty Range Rover and drove off.

'We showed 'em,' said Einstein, puffing out his already well-puffed chest.

'I'm not sure what we showed 'em,' replied Tom.

'That we won't take no shit!'

Tom opened his mouth to respond but Gillian interrupted. 'Guys, I've had it. We need to discuss how this went, but not today.'

Tom nodded. 'Anyone up for a burger, then?'

'I'd rather a nice seafood buffet,' said Gillian, wiping perspiration from her forehead. 'And I could do with a decent Chardonnay.'

'You want seafood?' asked Einstein. 'I'll fix it up for Tuesday.'

Gillian looked surprised. 'Really? How nice of you, Mr Einfeld!'

Gillian, Tom and some of the others wandered off to get lunch. Emma didn't go with them so Jason headed home. He didn't feel like celebrating with the greenies anyway. After all, what had they really achieved?

Since the official decision about the logging was due soon, it wouldn't be long before they found out.

Chapter 4

Buffeted

Jason's bed was covered with fragments of a cardboard box and torn-apart plastic bags. Two instruction leaflets lay open on the desk and bits of computer were strewn across the floor.

'Typical,' said Jason, adjusting the tangle of connectors inside his computer. 'The graphics card arrives on the day I'm supposed to go to that thing with the greenies.'

'Then don't go,' said David.

'It's not as though I even agree with them. They could be wrong for all I know. Screwdriver.'

David passed the tool, then picked up a stray fan and inspected it. 'Shouldn't this have gone in there somewhere?'

'Couldn't see a place for it,' said Jason as he screwed the computer's case back together.

'Won't it blow up or something, if you don't do it right?'

'One way to find out.' Jason connected the peripherals and plugged in the power cord, but hesitated before flicking the switch on the power point. 'Come here.'

David looked half mystified and half distrustful, but complied. Jason positioned his bulky friend between himself and the computer, then snaked out a skinny arm towards the power point.

'Get lost,' protested David, twisting out of harm's way. He easily overpowered Jason and held Jason in front of himself.

'There's no point trying to use me as a shield. Most of you would stick out the sides.'

'Just turn it on, smart-arse.'

Jason did. The computer powered up normally.

Jason's antiquated version of *Grand Theft Auto* had never looked so good nor run so well. It was almost like driving on a real public road—not that Jason had ever been allowed to do that, despite much begging. The new graphics card was obviously a brute and would have no problems running even the latest version of the game, but unfortunately the rest of the computer wouldn't be up to the task.

Jason's mother popped her head around the bedroom door and frowned at the debris. 'I thought you two were going to do some homework.'

'We are,' said Jason. 'Computing. I showed David how to install a graphics card. We're just seeing if we got it right.'

Mrs Saunders tried to stifle a smile but failed. 'If you can stand to tear yourselves away from your work, there's something coming up on the news you might want to see.'

Jason looked down. That sort of invitation always brought back bad memories of grappling with the Prime Minister last year. The PM had decided Australia shouldn't have strict emission controls, which infuriated Jason because he was determined something should be done about global warming. Then, one evening, the man got caught in a rip while swimming near Sapphire Bay, and Jason managed to save him from drowning. When the PM promised Jason any reward he wanted, Jason asked him to agree to the emission controls. Even though that wasn't the sort of thing the politician had in mind, his promise was caught on tape by reporters so he was trapped.

Things got pretty messy after that. It was on TV a lot, and Jason was harassed by reporters so much that he eventually caved in and let the PM do whatever he wanted. The PM finally *did* approve the emission controls, but even though the politician made up his own mind in the end, Jason still got blamed for it so he'd learnt to ignore the issue when it was on TV and in the paper. But his mum still pointed out any mentions of it.

Jason and David followed Mrs Saunders into the lounge room. Jason's father was lying on a lounge chair that was reclined so far back he would have been staring at the ceiling if he hadn't had his hands behind his head.

After an ad break, the news resumed:

In the face of the economic downturn, the Prime Minister, Graham Lindsay, has come under fire for his continued support of the Rotterdam emission control targets. The Australian Business Council has claimed that the restrictions are crippling the Australian economy because local businesses can't compete with those in countries that didn't sign up to the

Rotterdam targets. It also pointed out that because the world's biggest polluters didn't sign up, Australia's efforts to cut emissions will not significantly reduce global warming.

In a statement issued earlier today, Mr Lindsay had this to say: 'It's true that the Rotterdam proposals haven't been as widely accepted as we would have liked. The government understands the challenges that Australian industry is facing and is considering options to assist. We'll be making a major announcement shortly.'

David blew a raspberry. 'They didn't mention you.'

'Why should they?' replied Jason. 'I didn't force the PM to agree to those emission controls.'

'You did at the start.'

'That was before they showed me that everything's too complicated and isn't any of my business.'

'So old Graham's going to make a major announcement, is he?' murmured Mr Saunders. 'It had better be good. Else there'll be one less fish processing factory by the end of the year: mine.'

Jason's mother pointed at the clock on the wall. 'You'd better get moving, Jason. You don't want to be late for your dinner.'

'I don't think I'll go,' said Jason, waving an arm at the TV. 'That's reminded me why I didn't want to get involved in the first place.'

Mrs Saunders frowned. 'I think you should go. It'd do you good.'

'And don't forget Emma will be there,' added David, starting his eyebrow thing again.

Jason's mother looked quizzically at David but didn't follow up on his comment. 'Aren't they having a seafood buffet? That's good for Dad's business. Especially if it's somewhere nice, like Hendrick's.'

Mr Saunders grunted. 'Can you get them to have one every night?'

'I guess I did win against the PM,' said Jason. 'Oh well, if they really want to know why their march sucked, I can tell them.' He got up and headed to his room.

'Put on some proper clothes,' his mother called after him. 'Hendrick's won't let you in if you're wearing jeans.'

●　　●　　●

The caravan park was pretty dead at this time of year. Jason cycled slowly towards a cabin that had a pair of jeans drying on a makeshift clothes line, propped his bike against a nearby gum tree, then peered through the fly screen door. Gillian and a few of the other greenies were inside. Gillian gestured for Jason to join them.

'How's our political strategist?' she asked. 'All dressed up for the occasion, I see.'

'So we're going to Hendrick's?' asked Jason.

'Einstein's keeping it a secret. He just said for everyone to be here at six.'

Gillian's cabin wasn't much bigger than a caravan, and was boringly tidy. Other than the jeans outside, the only sign that someone was actually living there was a set of ornaments lined up neatly along the edge of the orange kitchen bench.

Through the window that comprised one end of the cabin, Jason could see several groups of greenies walking across from the camping area on the other side of the park.

A few cars drove up as well. Soon the cabin was full, and new arrivals congregated in the canvas annex attached to its side. Everyone was dressed nicely, which didn't look right at all.

Jason kept an eye out for Tom's delivery van, but Tom arrived in a Nissan X-Trail. Unfortunately, he seemed to be on his own, except for a yellow Labrador that started to show an interest in a large pot plant near the cabin door.

Gillian caught sight of the dog and rushed over with arms flailing. 'Get lost, you nuisance!'

'It's not mine, your honour,' said Tom. 'Or were you talking to me?'

'Its owners just let it roam around off its leash. I've got a good mind to slap a cease-and-desist order on them.'

Tom sighed. 'Typical barrister,' he said with a smile.

Jason thought about that. 'Barista. Isn't that someone who makes coffee?'

'I do *not* make coffee,' Gillian answered testily. 'I'm a *barrister*, a lawyer. Just because I'm a woman, everyone assumes—'

Tom interrupted, flicking one of the pot plant's leaves. 'Maybe we should find a better place for this.'

'I've got a philodendron by my front door in Sydney, so I put one here too since I thought this was going to be home for a while. But after last weekend….'

The lawyer didn't finish her sentence because she was distracted by a dirty Ford Escort ute that was driving way too fast through the caravan park. It headed straight for Gillian's cabin but at the last second skidded to a halt with all four wheels locked, spewing a cloud of dust into the air.

Gillian looked terrified and furious at the same time, but Tom just bashed his forehead with his hand and muttered 'Einstein'.

As the dust cleared, Einstein's grinning face appeared through the driver's side window. 'Seafood buffet time!'

Gillian's expression changed to resignation. 'I'll get my handbag,' she said, and turned to go inside.

'You don't need no handbag,' said Einstein. He got out of the car, revealing a dirty singlet, stubbies and bare feet. After gathering up a mound of paper parcels from the floor of the vehicle, he strode past Gillian into the cabin. A similarly-clad passenger got out of the other side of the ute and lugged an esky in, leaving a trail of sand on the lino. Gillian quickly tended to it with a dustpan and broom.

'Hey, city-girl,' called Einstein, 'this is the coast. It's *supposed* to be bloody sandy.' With a sweep of his arm, he shoved the ornaments on the kitchen bench to one side and dropped his parcels in their place. He tore into one, revealing an oily mound of battered fish. A second parcel became a mountain of chips.

Gillian shook her head slowly and smiled, then took a stack of plastic plates down from an overhead cupboard and placed them on the bench. 'I'm not sure whether I've got enough crockery for everyone.'

'I reckon you do, since we don't need none,' said Einstein, ripping off a piece of butchers' paper and dumping a generous handful of chips onto it. Gillian took a plate but most of the others made do with paper. Jason opted for paper as well, figuring it was somehow better for the environment. Recycling, or something.

'Okay, where's my Chardonnay?' asked Gillian. Einstein's accomplice opened the esky and tossed her a can of something that almost certainly wasn't Chardonnay.

Jason dug around inside the esky and was surprised to find a lemonade. He retreated to a corner of the cabin and sat on the scratchy brown material that substituted for carpet. The eating arrangements made it impossible to eat politely; a chunk of fish escaped down the front of his good shirt, leaving a greasy trail. Mum wasn't going to be impressed, but it was her fault for making him dress up in the first place.

Tom saw Jason eating on his own and came over to pass on an apology from Emma. She'd wanted to come so she could thank Jason for going on the march, but her mother had grounded her. Tom also took the opportunity to ask Jason if he'd seen Sal recently, but he hadn't. Apparently nobody had seen Sal since the protest rally. His car and things were still in the caravan park so it wasn't as though he'd just left without telling anyone.

Jason was itching to find out why Emma had been grounded but he knew it was none of his business. He was about to ask Tom about his computer problem when Gillian called him away. Targeting Tom's computer was a sure sign the loggers were up to something weird, but what was also weird was that Emma didn't seem to think anything needed to be done about it.

Just as Jason was helping himself to a second piece of fish, Gillian's mobile rang and she hustled off to the bedroom to take the call. Jason tried not to listen in but couldn't help overhearing some of the conversation since his niche was near the bedroom door. 'Already?' he heard Gillian say. 'I didn't expect it so soon.' When she emerged, she looked like she might have heard about a death in the family. Tom asked if she was okay; she replied with a nod but didn't look very happy.

After everyone had finished eating, Gillian called them all into the annex. There weren't enough folding chairs to go around, so most people just sat on the tarpaulin floor. Now that the sun had set, it was surprisingly cool. Jason wished he'd brought a hoodie. While he waited for everyone to settle down, he rehearsed in his mind what he planned to tell them about their lame march. The tricky part was how to say it politely.

Gillian tapped on one of the annex's poles to get everyone's attention, then thanked them for coming. 'I was really hoping Sal would be here, but we'll have to start without him. I think we all know that our protest march could have gone better.'

'Whaddaya mean?' interrupted Einstein. 'We kicked their arse. I was on TV!'

'You don't get it, do you?' said a voice from the back of the annex. Einstein looked around with a fierce expression on his face but couldn't work out who'd spoken.

Gillian quickly continued. She read from a newspaper article that called the protest 'embarrassing' and her speech at the end of it 'a rambling shambles'. Jason silently agreed with those assessments. Gillian certainly didn't seem like she could convince a jury of anything. Maybe she wasn't a very good lawyer.

Gillian's focus dropped to the ground and she exhaled deeply. 'I was going to use those quotations to start a discussion on how we can do better next time. But during our, um, "seafood buffet", I received news from someone I know in the government.' She looked up at the group in front of her. 'The logging contract has been approved.'

Jason visualised the forest disappearing. And Emma with it.

Chapter 5

Animal Acts

The annex was silent. Everyone seemed stunned that it was all over so quickly. Einstein was the first to recover: 'But we haven't finished protesting yet!'

Gillian smiled slightly. 'They weren't waiting for us. They were waiting for the EIA—Environmental Impact Assessment report. And apparently that says it's okay for the loggers to go ahead.'

'We're screwed then,' said Tom.

'Game over,' said someone else. 'We might as well go home.'

That seemed to be the general feeling. Nobody thought there was much point discussing how to continue the fight since the fight had already been lost. The greenies finished their drinks in silence and, one by one, wandered off into the night. A few shook hands with one another before parting company.

After thanking Einstein for the fish and chips, and receiving a grunt in reply, Jason started pedalling home. He didn't quite know how to feel. While it was good to be off the hook, he couldn't help but feel sorry for the greenies. Of course, if that report said the logging was okay then it probably was, and the greenies were probably wrong. Probably. So many probablies. At least he could now go back to officially not having an opinion.

•   •   •

After a few days, the logging drama started to recede into the background of Jason's consciousness, leaving only the drudgery of school. In English, Ms Gow was trying to ram home the importance of that essential life skill, the book review. 'You *must* tell me what you thought of the book. Too many of your reviews didn't do that.'

Yeah yeah, thought Jason. The book was boring, but if he'd said that in his book review, he knew what sort of mark he'd have received. It was definitely safer not to have opinions.

He stealthily flipped open his phone, just in case he'd missed any messages from the greenies. He'd swung by the caravan park yesterday to see if those who were staying there had left. Most of them hadn't, because they'd already paid their rent up until the end of the week.

Ms Gow seemed to have a sixth sense about mobile phones. Maybe she could detect radio waves or something. 'Put that away, Jason. Your report needed *serious* work. You didn't tell me anything I couldn't have found out from the book's back cover.'

As soon as the teacher had diverted her glare, Jason felt a sharp stabbing pain between his shoulder blades. He spun around to see Emma, who was sitting behind him, withdrawing a ruler. 'Naughty boy,' she said under her breath.

'What about you?' retorted Jason. 'You were grounded and couldn't go to the greenies' thing.'

'Oh that.' Emma dismissed it with a wave. 'The dragon sprung me in one of the guest's rooms in her beloved bed-and-breakfast place. It's not as though I was nicking stuff.'

'Dragon?'

'Just some woman who's moved in with Dad at home.'

Emma suddenly looked towards the teacher. Jason figured it was because Ms Gow had latched onto their conversation so he quickly swung around and faked an interest in the book on his desk. But it was a false alarm; the teacher had her back to the class and was scrawling on the whiteboard.

'Did you hear about Sal?' whispered Emma. 'Someone tried to kill him, or slash him, or something. They smashed a window on his caravan with a log.'

'Holy crap! Is he okay?'

'He's alive. But he isn't coming back.'

Jason's mind flashed up images of the gorilla-like logger hacking into a piece of timber at the protest rally. It had to be him.

Something didn't add up, though. 'The loggers have already won!' said Jason. 'Why would they bother?'

'Maybe they did it before they found out they'd won.'

That was possible. So Sal got attacked for no reason. How stupid. It made as much sense as the virus on Tom's computer.

The news about Sal put an end to Jason's ability to concentrate on English or any other subject that day. More than usual, he looked forward to heading home and losing himself in *Grand Theft Auto*.

• • •

Finally the opportunity arrived. David came home with Jason, which was a bit embarrassing because it was cold inside. Mr Saunders wouldn't put the fire on because he was being tight about firewood.

Jason borrowed his father's laptop so he and David could go head-to-head. Even though the pair were totally familiar with all the roads in the game, there were still crashes. David was so good that Jason had to take heaps of risks just to give himself a chance of winning. Unfortunately, that tactic usually just resulted in specky rolls and spinouts accompanied by the scream of skidding tyres.

Jason took another corner too fast and his Chevy spun out again. This time, the screech of the tyres didn't seem to finish when it should have: even after the car slammed sideways into a building and stopped dead, the squeal continued.

Bewildered, Jason and David looked at one another until they realised the bogus sound was coming from outside. They rushed to the window just in time to see Einstein's derelict ute skid to a halt, its wheels slamming sideways into the curb harder than was probably good for them.

'Uh oh,' said Jason. 'I wonder what he wants.'

Jason opened the front door and a cold wind blasted in. Despite the weather, Einstein was wearing his usual khaki singlet, which made Jason feel even colder.

'You heard about Sal?' asked Einstein, although he made it sound more like a demand than a question.

Jason nodded.

'The meeting's back on. Gillian's place. Tomorrow night. Seven.'

'Why? I thought you'd lost.' Jason swallowed as soon as he'd spoken; a tactless comment like that could easily result in a physical reply.

The muscles in Einstein's shoulders twitched. 'Look kid, I still reckon you're useless but Gillian says we need you, so just be there. Got it?'

'Sure,' said Jason, nodding vigorously. 'You could have just called me.'

'People don't say "no" to me when I'm standing in front of them.' Einstein turned and stalked back to his ute.

Jason spent the rest of the evening wondering what was going on. Why were the greenies meeting again if the government had already made up its mind? Perhaps some new information had come to light. The loggers' victory did seem a bit too easy. They needn't have bothered maiming Sal, and attacking the greenies' computers seemed even more pointless. Maybe that's what Einstein's meeting was going to be about, although Einstein didn't seem like he'd even know how to turn a computer on.

● ● ●

None of the greenies seemed particularly surprised that Einstein was late to his own meeting. It was twenty past seven and there was still no sign of him.

Jason was glad Emma was there this time, even though he found it hard to figure her out. He wanted to ask why she'd broken into other people's rooms but wasn't sure how touchy she'd be about it. At least asking would have been less awkward than the long periods of silence in their conversation.

A screech outside signalled Einstein's arrival. Gillian called everyone into the annex then gestured for Einstein to speak.

'It's like this. Youse all know what them bastards done to Sal. We gotta fight them. Simple as that.'

The audience responded with calls of 'yeah' and 'right on'.

'We gotta break their legs,' continued Einstein.

A few of the greenies vocalised agreement but most didn't seem so keen.

'I don't think I'll be doing that,' said Tom.

'And I won't have anything to do with violence,' added Gillian. 'I *am* a lawyer, remember?'

Einstein reddened. 'What a bunch of gutless wonders! Youse said youse wanted to fight, so fight.'

'Not that way,' said Tom. 'Let's hit them where it'll hurt them: in their wallets.'

Gillian nodded. 'We might still be able to stop them from logging. That's what Sal wanted. Not broken bones.'

'Bloody wimps,' said Einstein. He strode through the group to the back of the annex and slumped onto the floor, worryingly close to Jason and Emma.

Nobody took over the meeting. The annex was silent, except for the splopping of raindrops on the canvas roof. If that didn't quit soon, it was going to be a wet ride home.

Tom poked Gillian in the shoulder with a pen, then repeated it. After a third prod, Gillian dragged herself out of her chair and turned to face everyone. 'I don't think I should be the one to organise our efforts any more. Just look at our protest last weekend. If I'd got that right, the logging might never have been approved.'

A messy debate broke out. Most of the greenies wanted Gillian to stay on as leader because she was an environmental lawyer, but Gillian kept quoting newspaper articles about how hopeless the protest march had been. Einstein occasionally snapped out of his sulking to agree with Gillian about how lousy she was.

Jason thought Gillian seemed pretty normal, which is more than could be said for most of the greenies. If she quit, they didn't stand much of a chance—especially if Einstein or one of his out-of-control mates took over. At one stage the lawyer looked around as though she was looking for a way out, and Jason found himself nodding to support her. He received a weak smile in reply.

Eventually, Gillian gave in to the majority view and agreed to carry on for a while. She didn't seem very happy about it, though. Neither did Einstein.

'Okay, I've been studying reports about our efforts so far,' said the lawyer. 'We need to do things a bit differently. I've boiled it down to two factors: *focus* and *evidence*.'

Tom opened a clipboard and started writing.

Gillian explained what she meant. At the protest march, the placards had been vague and against logging generally, and the speech had mentioned a lot of things but hadn't concentrated on anything in particular. What they needed to do was to pick a single reason why the logging should be stopped, and just use that for all their placards and posters and speeches. That way, the public could relate to the protest more easily since they'd only have to latch onto one thing.

Someone suggested the focus should be the loggers' greed since they wanted to sell the wood, but Gillian screwed up her face and picked up a thick soft-covered book. 'This is the report that recommends they log the forest. It's supposedly justified by ecological thinning considerations.'

Everyone said that was crap. Jason asked Emma what it meant, but Emma just shrugged.

'Do we have any evidence that it's not valid?' asked Gillian. 'Any data? Any analysis?'

The yabbering gave way to silence. Tom put his pen down.

'Unless we can lay our hands on some proof,' continued the lawyer, 'we'd need to pay a university to do a study on it. And that wouldn't be cheap.'

Jason's interest level jumped at the mention of data and analysis. Presumably the loggers already had some in their report. He started the browser in his phone and looked up 'logical thinning' in Wikipedia but there wasn't an entry for it.

'How about biodiversity?' said a voice from behind Jason.

Gillian tapped her fingers on the report. 'The Environmental Impact Assessment says there isn't any unusual wildlife in the forest. The birds are only common ones, and most of the native animals that used to be there have been displaced by rats and feral cats.'

'Isn't there some sort of marsupial?' asked someone. 'Not kangaroos; an endangered … something.'

Tom wrote that down on his clipboard but looked sceptical. 'I've never seen anything unusual, and I go walking there every day.'

A few other possibilities were discussed and Tom jotted them all down. Tom himself suggested tourism, since lots of the people who spent their holidays in Sapphire Bay went walking in the forest. If tourist attractions got destroyed, then less people would come to Sapphire Bay, meaning less money would be spent in the local businesses. Jason was very familiar with that argument since it was exactly what his father said.

After half an hour, everyone was out of ideas. The silence revealed that the rain had gone from splopping to steady. Jason regretted not moving his bike. There was nothing worse than cycling on a sodden bike-seat— especially when you had a perfectly good car sitting in a carport at home. Jason was in no doubt that he could drive around town perfectly safely, except for the silly legal requirements.

'You're being very quiet, Jason,' said Gillian.

Jason thought the most obvious thing to do was to prove that the loggers' thinning report was wrong, but based on his battle to convince the PM about climate change, he realised that would be easier said than done. Finding out about the mystery animal in the forest would be easier. But the close proximity of Einstein made it too risky to say anything, so he just shrugged.

Gillian had Tom read out the list of suggestions. 'We don't have to pick one tonight,' she said. 'Just think about it. And don't forget it has to be something we can get evidence for. And I mean *legally*, Einstein.'

Everyone got up, and most of them dashed off into the rainy darkness. Jason looked over to his dripping bike.

'I'll give you a lift,' said Tom. 'We can't have our most important member getting pneumonia.'

'Nobody will give a shit what the Boy Wonder says,' commented Einstein while struggling to extract his keys from his shorts. 'Everyone can see the kid's useless since the PM ditched that global warming stuff.'

'That isn't what happened!' Jason snapped back. 'I won.'

'Guess again.'

'Ignore him,' said Tom, turning away from Einstein's car to avoid the inevitable mud spray.

Jason nodded. 'What's wrong with your computer?'

'It's weird. Whenever I start the internet, it always goes to the logging company's page. And my calendar keeps opening up automatically, too.'

'I could look at it for you,' offered Jason.

Before Tom could answer, Emma did so for him. 'No need. It's nothing.'

Tom didn't get to argue his case because Gillian called him away. Jason looked at Emma, who looked down as usual. That was the second time she'd said there was nothing wrong with Tom's computer. Was she was trying to ensure Jason didn't go to her house? Maybe she didn't really like him at all, and was just using him to help get rid of the loggers.

There was another possibility: she could be on the loggers' side! Perhaps she knew what the loggers were up to with her father's computer and she didn't want Jason to figure it out. That seemed pretty improbable, but at least it wouldn't mean she was simply trying to avoid him.

While waiting for Tom to return, Jason flipped his phone open again and googled 'marsupial sapphire state forest', but nothing relevant came up. He wrinkled his nose and showed Emma the screen. 'Shame,' she said.

'I looked up "logical thinning" before and nothing came up for that, either.'

Emma's eyes narrowed. 'That doesn't sound right.' She walked over to Tom, who was in deep discussion with Gillian, and slid the clipboard out from under his arm.

Tom's notes were about as neat as Jason's schoolwork. Things were written all over the place, even sideways. 'EVIDENCE' was scrawled in huge letters across the bottom of the page and underlined three times.

'There,' said Emma, pointing at the middle of the page. 'It's ECOlogical thinning.'

'Ohhh. So it isn't logical, then.'

When Tom returned, the three of them went out into the rain and pushed Jason's bike into the back of Tom's van, then squeezed side-by-side into the front. Being squeezed beside Emma wasn't entirely unpleasant.

'Do you know why Einstein visited everyone before this meeting, instead of ringing them?' asked Tom as they drove off. 'It's because he just got a new mobile and can't figure out how to use it.'

Jason and Emma laughed. Laughing with Emma felt good too.

'Einstein … is a worry,' said Jason.

Tom exhaled slowly. 'Gillian and I were just discussing what to do about him. She's asked me to keep an eye on him. So let me know if he does anything stupid.'

●　　●　　●

It was about 9pm when Jason got home. He headed straight for his bedroom, where debris from his computer upgrade still littered the floor. He tiptoed through the mess and flicked the machine on.

There had to be something on the internet about what animals were in Sapphire Forest, but it wasn't easy find out what. Depending on how Jason specified the search, he got either thousands of irrelevant hits or none at all. Maybe Sapphire Forest was too small to have good information on the internet. Maybe the government just didn't care about it, which would explain why they were letting the loggers cut it down. But if there really were endangered animals in there, that was a pretty sick thing to do. And not in a good way.

Just as Jason was about to direct Google's attention to ecological thinning, his mother stuck her head around the door and frowned at the lack of visible carpet. 'So how are you taking the news?' she asked.

'What news?'

'Oh, maybe you didn't hear. Mr Lindsay has pulled out of the Rotterdam emission control agreement.'

Chapter 6

Poo

Jason wondered if he'd heard correctly. Sure, people had been hassling the PM to bail out of the Rotterdam agreement, but that wasn't anything new. Jason never thought he'd actually do it.

Jason's mother was still standing in the doorway, obviously expecting some sort of response.

'So he's not going to reduce Australia's emissions?' asked Jason. 'He's going to allow global warming?'

Mrs Saunders nodded.

'Oh.' Jason swallowed. 'Well, it's his decision, I guess.' He pivoted on his chair and turned his attention back to his computer screen.

'I know this means a lot to you, Jason. I'm sorry—'

'No it doesn't. He's probably right. It's too complicated for me.'

Jason's mother looked at him in silence for a while, then left.

Jason told himself that he shouldn't be surprised. Mr Lindsay had never really wanted to sign up to the

Rotterdam agreement. Not at first, anyway. He probably only did it to get the reporters to stop saying he was ungrateful after Jason had saved his life.

Jason tried to put the issue out of his mind, and resumed googling for animals in Sapphire Forest. Unfortunately, the search engine seemed more interested in trying to sell him sapphire jewellery. Maybe if he just bought something, it would be satisfied and tell him what he wanted to know. Perhaps Emma would like a nice sapphire pendant or something.

After a few more attempts, he gave up. There just didn't seem to be any useful info about the forest. Plus, it was hard to concentrate when the PM had just decided to destroy the environment.

Why had Mr Lindsay chickened out now? Jason reasoned it would be okay to look up the story, just to check the facts. It wouldn't mean he had an opinion about it.

The issue was at the top of www.abc.net.au/news:

The Prime Minister, Mr Lindsay, has rescinded Australia's commitment to the emission control targets tabled at the Rotterdam Environmental Conference last year. The move has been applauded by industry groups, who have been lobbying the government to reconsider its policy in light of the ongoing economic downturn. However, environmentalists have slammed the decision. The PM defended his change of heart at a press conference this afternoon:

'The Rotterdam targets didn't get as much traction as we'd hoped. Many countries declined to adopt them, and that includes several of Australia's most important

trading partners and allies. We have to take into account that Australia is just one of about 200 countries, and our population is less than half a percent of the world's total. If the world's largest countries maintain their emissions at current levels, global warming will happen whether Australia sticks to the Rotterdam targets or not.'

Great, thought Jason. *Everyone else is doing it, so we might as well.* He thumped his computer's power button in disgust, then remembered he wasn't supposed to care.

'It doesn't matter,' he said loudly, even though there was nobody else in the room. 'I don't mind.' He glanced towards the door in case his outburst had attracted his parents' attention, but he seemed to have gotten away with it.

A *Science Adviser* magazine crunched beneath him as he flopped backwards onto his bed without looking. He fished it out and perused the contents page.

'I can guess what you don't mind,' said Mr Saunders, helping himself to a corner of the bed.

'No need. You're probably glad about it. You never wanted emission controls 'cause they were bad for your business.'

'Well, yeah.' Jason's father poked at the box from Jason's new graphics card with one of his ugg boots. 'This family needs all the money it can get so we can keep you in computers.'

Jason screwed up his nose.

'Are you sure you don't want to talk about this?' asked Mr Saunders awkwardly. D&M just wasn't his thing.

'No, it's cool,' replied Jason. 'Global warming's cool.'

Jason's father didn't look convinced, but left anyway.

• • •

Instead of getting out of bed on Saturday morning, Jason just lay there. He couldn't see a lot of point to getting up.

But his stomach didn't see it that way, and demanded satisfaction. Surprisingly, the house was toasty warm; Dad must have caved in and authorised use of the fireplace. Now, all of a sudden, there was global warming *and* local warming.

After breakfast, Jason sat in front of his computer Wikipedia-ing random things that didn't really interest him. It passed the time, even if it meant wasting the weekend. Wasting a weekend was nothing, since the whole of the last Christmas holidays ended up being wasted. All that time spent playing the PM's silly little games, dodging nosey reporters and pushy locals—all for nothing, because the PM simply changed his mind.

Jason's moping was continually interrupted by his mother, who was flitting around and being over-the-top upbeat. It was obviously an act intended to cheer him up but it actually made him feel worse because it emphasised that he *needed* cheering up.

When he couldn't take any more of his mother's high spirits, Jason took himself off to the beach. Not the main swimming beach, but the quiet beach where he went to think.

And where he'd saved the Prime Minister from drowning, starting off this whole mess.

In the aftermath of the lifesaving incident, Jason had wielded a lot of influence over the PM. He tried to work out how he could get that influence back. Maybe he should spend all his spare time hanging around the beach in case the politician was silly enough to swim into a rip again.

The ocean was drab grey under an overcast sky. If anyone had been out there in this weather, it would have been impossible to see them since the wind was whipping up foam as far out as the eye could see.

Mr Lindsay wasn't likely to get caught in a rip again anyway. He will have learnt his lesson. The PM got the better deal out of the episode since his lesson was a good thing to know, while Jason had learnt he was stupid and should butt out. If there'd been any lingering doubt about that, the PM's recent decision took it away.

Jason realised coming to this beach was a mistake. It would always be a reminder of his failure. He'd have to find a new place to think.

But not today. It was too cold. Figuring that his mother should have settled down by now, Jason trudged back home. As he walked up the driveway, he came face to face with his Predator, which was resting quietly in the carport. The vehicle was proof that the PM was actually a good bloke, so long as you didn't care about global warming, since he gave it to Jason as a reward for saving his life—even though he also gave in to Jason's request for emission controls. At least for a while.

Not having emission controls any more would have some advantages, Predator-wise. Since carbon dioxide pollution was officially Not A Problem any more, Jason wouldn't have to feel guilty about driving. Plus, the petrol money his father forked over (after a lot of whinging) would last a bit longer since petrol would be cheaper.

Suddenly Jason had an appalling thought: what if Mr Lindsay wanted to take the Predator back now? Since he suddenly seemed happy to forget about everything they'd gone through, his next decision could be to reclaim the vehicle.

That would be sad.

The greenies wouldn't be sad about it, of course. They were pretty insistent that burning petrol for fun was a bad idea, even though Einstein did it. But then, what the greenies thought would be irrelevant to Jason from now on, since they wouldn't want a loser like him to be involved with them any more. Einstein, of all people, was right about that. Since Jason had failed to get the PM to adopt emission controls after all, he wouldn't make a very good representative for them. They'll just quietly drop him and have nothing more to do with him.

In a way, maybe everything was going to work out. He never really wanted to get dragged into the greenies' battle, and now he'd be out of it. Maybe he was entering a new form of existence in which everyone ignored him and didn't care what he did. Or what he didn't.

• • •

It had been a looong weekend, even though it was just the usual two days. Jason had tried to distract himself with *Grand Theft Auto* but he was just too familiar with his old version of it. For the first time that he could remember, he was glad when Monday rolled around. Even though school wasn't fun or interesting, at least it was something to do.

Not that there was any point paying attention or doing work. When you're useless and can't make any difference, it doesn't matter if you learn anything or not. School was therefore totally irrelevant.

Jason had no choice but to point this out to Ms Gow during English, when she wouldn't let him just sit there in peace.

'Forget about your politics,' said the teacher. 'We're talking about communication.'

'No point communicating,' replied Jason. 'Nobody's listening. Nobody gives a— Nobody cares.'

A husky voice from the back of the room said 'yeah'. Jason figured it was probably Bull. This must be the first time the thug had agreed with anything Jason said. If Jason's new attitude meant a reduced risk of attack from Bull, that would be a plus.

• • •

Maybe Bull didn't need to be avoided any more, but now Jason had to make sure he didn't run into Emma. Like the other greenies, she'd think he was a loser and he didn't want to hear her say it. He tried to convince himself that she mightn't care that the only justification for his existence had vaporised. After all, one shouldn't always fear the worst because the worst doesn't always happen. Unfortunately, he was no more successful in convincing himself than he was of convincing anybody else.

Jason managed to avoid Emma for almost the whole week, but he wasn't quite fast enough in escaping the classroom after maths on Friday. 'Hey you,' she said, tapping him on the shoulder.

Jason reluctantly stopped and turned around, looking her in the shoes. Judging by the rugby-striped socks in the shoes beside hers, David was there too.

'Got something for you,' said Emma. 'Hold out your hand.'

Jason complied, wondering where this was going. A present, perhaps? Something to show she still liked him despite the PM's bombshell? A stifled snigger from David heightened the mystery.

Emma unrolled a Ziploc bag and emptied its contents onto Jason's hand, while David burst into unrestrained laughter.

It took Jason a few seconds to recognise what he'd been given.

It was dog poo.

Chapter 7

Poo Power

Jason stared at the mess in his hand. If there'd been any doubt about what Emma thought of him now, this eliminated it. David, who was still giggling away, obviously wasn't interested in being supportive either.

Jason's natural instinct to drop the gift to the floor was balanced by the feeling that he'd got exactly what he deserved. He could even keep it as a memento of Emma, since it would be the only present he'd ever get from her.

'Be careful with that,' said Emma. 'It's valuable.'

What kind of sick joke was that? Did she mean it was more than he deserved? Probably. He let the brown lumps fall, then pivoted and strode off.

Heavy footsteps were gaining on him from behind. Jason broke into a run, and the following feet did likewise.

'Hey, wait up!' called David, but Jason didn't. He might have been useless from the neck up, but at least he was fit from swimming. Outrunning the lumbering David was no challenge. Just in case the fitter-looking Emma was a threat, Jason kept up a fast pace and didn't stop until he was well away from school.

• • •

Jason skipped his afternoon classes and stayed home. Fortunately it was one of his mother's work days so he had the place to himself until almost dinner time.

Even though dinner was fish and chips in front of the TV, Jason only sampled a few chips before retreating back to his room. He had to close the door to muffle the annoying exuberance of the game show his parents were watching. However, he only got through a couple of articles in his *Science Adviser* before his concentration was interrupted by raised voices.

'You did *what?*' Mr Saunders' voice was nearly screeching.

The reply was too quiet to make out, but it was a man's voice. It sounded like there was sobbing too.

Jason opened his bedroom door a couple of centimetres and put his eye to the gap. In the entry hall, his father was talking animatedly to someone at the front door, but his back was blocking Jason's view of the recipient of the lecture.

No, recipients plural. There were at least two men; maybe three.

One of the visitors leaned sideways and looked into the house. 'There he is,' he said. It was Einstein's voice.

Jason didn't know whether to retreat, keep listening or come out. Then another head peered around Mr Saunders. The silver-grey hair glowing in the harsh porch light was obviously Tom's. The final face to appear was Emma's.

And it had tears on it.

Emma's tears compelled Jason to venture forward. As he did so, Tom manoeuvred his daughter out from behind him.

'I'm sorry,' said Emma, without looking Jason in the face. 'But it was quoll poo.'

Jason wasn't sure what a quoll was, or why it should make any difference. 'It was still poo,' he replied.

'You don't get it. It was from the forest. Maybe from a rare quoll, the sort they thought was extinct.'

Jason thought about that. 'Quoll poo,' he said slowly. 'But why did you—'

'I was excited and wanted to show you. David told me to put it in your hand. He thought it would be funny.'

Jason rolled his eyes. That had a strong ring of truth to it. Typical David.

Emma held up the plastic bag she'd had at school. 'Isn't it great?' she asked, admiring the bag's contents. 'Dad found it.'

Jason instinctively took a step back when he saw the bag, but then moved in for a closer look. 'Okay, what's it for? How do you use it?'

'You don't use poo, stupid,' said Einstein, looking over Emma's shoulder.

'We're going to use this poo!' Tom replied. 'We're going to drop the loggers right in it.'

Chapter 8

Spiralling

It was going to be a long wait before they found out whether the droppings Tom had found were really from an endangered quoll. The sample had been sent off to a laboratory for testing. Jason thought it was a bit bizarre that the quolls' lives depended on their poo, but then his relationship with Emma now seemed to be based on the same substance.

The buzz over Tom's discovery contrasted starkly with the boringness of school. Or at least the lessons were boring; sometimes strange stuff happened around them. For example, on Wednesday, Jason hadn't felt like hanging out with anyone before school so he'd gone straight to his Civics classroom. As he drifted by the teacher's desk, he noticed Bull's nickname cut into the green vinyl. Did Bull really think it was so clever to do that? Couldn't anyone do it?

Jason took his lunch box out of his backpack and opened it. As expected, there was an orange—and a knife to peel it with. Nobody else was around, so he etched

'LIKES BOYS' below Bull's mark. By the time he'd finished, his heart was pounding.

Ms Cruikshank noticed the new addition as soon as she arrived. She refused to start the class until the culprit owned up. Someone tried to tell her it had been there for ages and she just hadn't noticed it before.

'Rubbish,' she snapped. 'It said "BULL" before, but what's below it is new. The shavings are still here so it must have been done this morning.'

Bugger, thought Jason, making a mental note to dispose of the evidence more thoroughly next time.

The teacher tried to find out who 'BULL' was but nobody dared to tell her. Jason stole a sideways glance at Bull. The bully was doing a great job of looking as disinterested as usual, even though he probably wanted to know who committed the act even more than the teacher did.

'Okay everyone,' said Ms Cruikshank, 'I've just decided there'll be another assignment.'

Groans from the class. Many rolled eyeballs.

'Tough. I want a 1,000-word essay from everyone on the social consequences of vandalism. You've got one week.'

Having dealt with the incident to her satisfaction, Ms Cruikshank launched into the lesson: a double period about discrimination. It was all totally obvious: judge everyone on their own merits, don't disadvantage anyone just because they belong to a particular group, yada yada yada. Some of the examples were a bit surprising though; for example, in a war, it's illegal to attack an enemy town even though some of their people attacked you first. That's called *collective punishment* and is against the Geneva

Convention. Since most of the people in the town didn't attack you, they shouldn't have to suffer.

One of the students asked about global warming, pointing out that some countries pollute more than others but everyone's going to suffer for it. Ms Cruikshank didn't think that was an example of discrimination, even though it was like nature was going to punish everyone for what a few countries were doing. Jason figured Mr Lindsay would have agreed with the teacher.

Even though she was pooey with the class, Ms Cruikshank still let them have a break between periods. Jason noticed that Bull headed straight for the teacher's desk. While it would have been interesting to see his reaction, Jason deemed it safer to leave the room like everyone else.

After the break, Bull was sitting on Jason's desk. 'Get us out of this extra assignment, Saunders, or you're dead.'

'Why me?' asked Jason, trying to seem surprised even though his whole body was shaking.

Bull tapped the front of Jason's folder, where his name was: 'J. SAUNDƐRS'.

Jason still didn't get it. 'So?'

Bull tapped the 'Ɛ' firmly. 'You're the only one who does stupid Es like that. Either this assignment goes or I'll see you after school.'

Jason collapsed onto his chair. *Crap*. There's another tip for the future: *don't use your own writing style*. Maybe there was more to vandalism than he first thought. Now he was going to get the crap thrashed out of him unless he could get everyone out of the essay.

The obvious thing to do was to fess up, but if the incident got back to Mr Saunders it would probably result in a cuff on the side of the head and perhaps even a suspension of petrol money. But maybe there was another way….

Ms Cruikshank was about to get started after the break when Jason put up his hand. 'I don't think I fully got what you were saying about discrimination.'

The teacher looked surprised. 'What's your problem, Mr Saunders?'

'Are you saying we shouldn't treat people as though they've done something wrong when they haven't?'

'I'd have thought that was obvious.'

'I'm confused about this new assignment. We didn't all write on your desk. Only one person did, probably. Is it okay for you to make *all* of us do extra work because of that? Isn't that collective punishment?'

Ms Cruikshank glared at Jason, who could feel his head turning red. He wanted to look away but didn't want to appear as though he was up to something.

'The assignment is cancelled,' said the teacher tersely. 'I don't care; it saves me marking them. But if I find out who did this….'

Jason sat down without a word. He felt hot enough to vomit. Even though he'd managed to avoid a thrashing, something still felt unresolved about the incident. Five minutes later, he realised what it was: Bull was concerned about getting out of an assignment but didn't seem to care about what Jason had written about him. That was interesting.

Jason's next class was supposed to be maths, followed by IT. He skipped them both since he now realised there was no point getting good marks. He could pass those subjects without trying. The only problem was his parents, who were disappointed that his marks this year were a lot worse than last year.

Instead of following the drones to class, Jason made his way to the most secluded computer in the library. The school's network had heaps of software he didn't have at home, and he figured he learnt more from hacking around on computers than from copying down whiteboards of equations.

The final period of the day was English. Jason wasn't sure whether he still went to English because there was a chance he might fail it or because Emma was in the same class. Today, it would have been better if Emma hadn't been there because she saw the mark on his most recent essay: 3/10. Jason didn't respond to her tutting.

3/10! What was wrong with it? Jason read Ms Gow's comment: 'Once again, you've failed to draw any conclusions. You've summarised the facts but didn't tell me what you thought.'

Ms Gow didn't get it. His essay was perfect. He'd expressed his opinions to exactly the extent to which they were valuable. Deliberately.

'Sorry about your essay,' said Emma after class, as they trudged down the stairwell.

'I'll give Gow the Sow an opinion. I think she's a bitch.'

'Gow the Sow,' repeated Emma, smirking. 'She isn't *that* bad.'

'At least I won't have to put up with her in debating, since I've quit it.'

Emma looked confused. 'But wouldn't debating help you pass English? Doesn't it make you say your opinions?'

'That's just it. I can't do that and I shouldn't do that.'

After exiting the school building, Emma and Jason went their separate ways. As usual, Jason cut across the oval, towards the school's large roadside sign. He'd almost reached the sign when he noticed Bull leaning against it. There weren't any convenient bushes to disappear behind, so he altered course and walked as swiftly and quietly as he could.

It didn't work, though. 'Saunders, come here.'

Maybe if he pretended not to hear, and just kept going....

Bull repeated his demand.

Jason stopped. So he was going to be pulped after all. 'Oh, hi Bull. Didn't see you there.'

'Come. Here.'

Jason walked over as slowly as he dared. 'You said you weren't going to get me if I got you out of that assignment, and I did.'

'Yup. That was brill. Way to stuff up and get out of it.'

'Sooo,' said Jason, no longer sure where this was going.

'So, me and Greasy are going to nick this sign after the last bus. Wanna help?'

Never having been invited to such an event before, Jason didn't know quite how to respond. 'Um, no. I've got something on. But thanks.'

'Suit yourself,' said Bull. He turned to examine the bolts that were holding the sign in place.

Jason resumed a fast pace towards home. However, after a few strides, curiosity got the better of him. 'Um, Bull, what do you want the sign for?'

'Don't.'

'Then…'

Bull stopped poking at the structure and looked thoughtful. 'Proves I can do stuff. They reckon I can't, but this'll show them.'

Jason nodded and headed off again. In a twisted sort of way, Bull's answer actually made sense.

●   ●   ●

On Saturday, David came over for a hooning session but Jason didn't feel like doing anything fun. Not that McKenzie's field was that much fun any more, because the track was just too familiar. Jason could have driven it blindfolded. Plus, he'd already used up most of his monthly fuel allowance, which got smaller every time the cost of petrol went up. Jason had argued that the allowance should be measured in litres and not dollars, but his father had countered by suggesting that Jason should get a part-time job. Checkmate.

As usual, David seemed to be deaf to the word 'no'. Jason didn't have the energy to argue with him. They got into the Predator, and Jason started the engine. If he turned right, he'd go through the private gate to the neighbour's paddock, but if he went straight, he'd be on the public road. A few months ago, he'd driven to McKenzie's paddock via the road, but his father had found out and banned him from driving for a month—even though he was only on the road for fifty metres or so.

Still, it was tempting. All that asphalt with no traffic on it, just going to waste. Since Mr Lindsay was going to take the car back anyway, there was nothing to lose.

'What are we waiting for?' asked David.

'Nothing,' replied Jason, turning right.

David had first go around the track. For a bulked-up rugby player, he was a pretty tame driver. The tyres hardly ever left the dirt, even when the SUV bounded over the mound Mr McKenzie had been kind enough to dump near the end of the long straight section.

Jason's mind wandered back to Bull and his warped logic. So wrecking things was Bull's way of showing that he could make a difference. At least he *had* a way, thought Jason. It was probably better than contemplating your own uselessness all the time.

'Is Bull really so stupid?' said Jason, without really intending to say it out loud.

'Yes,' replied David emphatically. 'He's got so many loose screws it's a wonder he hasn't fallen apart.'

'Maybe that's why he wanted the bolts from the school's sign.'

'You were in on that?' asked David as he guided them sedately around a bend. 'If you go to jail, whose car could I thrash?'

'This isn't thrashing. Pull over and I'll show you thrashing.'

Jason drifted and fishtailed around the track, turning the air red with dust. There was silence from the passenger's seat. Jason glanced over and saw his friend gripping the dashboard with both hands, his eyes wide open.

David detected the glance and spoke up. 'Having fun?' he asked sarcastically.

'It's not about fun. It's about— I don't know what it's about.'

Even driving didn't take Jason's mind off other things. The Predator actually made things worse because it was a reminder he'd caved in to the PM. If he'd stuck to his guns, maybe Mr Lindsay would have had to keep his promise and agree to emission controls, and in that case he couldn't simply change his mind because then he'd be breaking the promise. So if Jason hadn't wimped out, maybe there'd still be emission controls.

Jason pushed the car harder and harder, as though punishing it for his own failure.

'Um, Jase?' said David. 'I don't have a death-wish.'

'Better get one.' Jason accelerated into a bend. The Predator started to tip to the left, forcing him to straighten the steering wheel even though that meant going off the side of the track. As soon as the vehicle thumped back to the ground, Jason pulled it back onto the track and floored it again.

'If you're going to keep driving like this, you can let me out now,' said David.

'That wasn't my fault. There's too much weight in the passenger's seat.'

'This isn't funny, Jason.'

By now they were in the long straight that lead to the jump. Jason grimly powered towards the mound, even though there was a turn just after it.

'Let me out,' demanded David, but Jason ignored him. The SUV traced a parabola through the air until the front bumper dug into a pile of rubble at the side of the track. Despite Jason's frantic steering, the car bounced on random wheels and glanced a tree. All the driver could do was to stand on the brakes. The vehicle skidded to a halt, facing back the way it had come.

The boys got out, and Jason walked around to the passenger's side to see if the encounter with the tree had done much damage. The grit in the air made him cough. David covered his nose with his handkerchief.

'Come on, you can breathe dirt, can't you?' said Jason.

David took the handkerchief from his face and held it up. Its centre was soaked with blood, and more was streaming from his nose. He strode towards the gate and didn't look back.

Chapter 9

Einstein's Mouth

It took the greenies a while to organise another protest march. As Jason approached the forming-up area on the appointed day, they still didn't look ready. For a start, many of the placards didn't have anything written on them. One of the greenies had a paint brush but she wasn't doing any painting.

'It's got to be about quolls,' Gillian was saying. 'That's what we're focusing on.'

'Sapphire Quoll Union Against Thinning: SQUAT,' suggested someone. 'Because we might have to stop the loggers by having a sit-in protest in the forest.'

A few people sniggered, but Gillian didn't like it. 'People might say we've got SQUAT. In fact, they already have been.'

Someone else offered 'FAQE: Friends Against Quoll Extinction.'

Tom looked uncomfortable. 'We don't want people saying our case is FAQE either,' he said. 'And don't forget that these quolls, "eastern quolls", were only thought to be extinct on the mainland. If the loggers wipe them out from here, there'll still be some elsewhere.'

'It's hard coming up with Q words,' complained the suggester. 'Couldn't you find some droppings from a dodo, or Tasmanian tiger, or something?'

Jason sidled up to Emma, who was scribbling on a sheet of paper. 'Sapphire Eastern Quoll Union to End Logging,' she'd written.

'That's clever,' whispered Jason. 'Tell them.'

'This is our second protest, so it's a SEQUEL,' Emma whispered back.

'Tell them,' repeated Jason, but Emma shook her head and gave Jason the sheet.

Jason didn't want to speak up either. He still wasn't convinced he should be at the protest at all, now that the PM had decided to disregard him. Gillian had said that that made him even more valuable to them because he was now like a downtrodden underdog, ignored for the sake of money. Just like the Sapphire Forest quolls.

The lawyer saw Emma hand over her page, so Jason held it up. 'Too long,' was the response.

'Quoll Action Party,' replied Jason so quickly that he surprised even himself.

'Excellent,' said Tom. 'Reflects the nature of the evidence.'

Gillian smiled and nodded. Everyone else liked QAP too, so they started daubing the blank placards with the new acronym.

'Smarty-pants,' said Emma, pinching Jason hard on the shoulder.

It hurt, but a pinch had never felt so good.

The protesters shuffled along the same route as before. Even though it looked like it might rain, there were heaps more spectators this time. News about the quolls had obviously got around, vindicating Gillian's decision to focus on that issue alone. The chanting was about quolls and all the placards and banners were about quolls; Tom had one that said 'QUOLLITY OF LIFE' and Emma's said 'EQUOLL RIGHTS'.

Now that Sal had left, someone else was leading the march. Jason thought they were pretty brave to take it on, after what had happened to Sal—not that anyone seemed to know exactly what that was. The new guy no where near as 'out there' as Sal but was doing an okay job. Unlike last time, some of the crowd were even joining in with the protesters' chant.

Even though he didn't want the loggers to wipe out the quolls, Jason still didn't want to be a public spectacle. He drifted towards the centre of the pack and only paid lip service to the shouting and arm-waving going on around him.

Unfortunately, Einstein looked around every so often to make sure everyone was putting in. Jason tried to look fired up whenever he detected Einstein's scans but he wasn't always fast enough. Angry gestures told Jason to punch the air like everyone else. He quickly complied.

A tap on the shoulder made him jump. 'Don't worry about Einstein,' said Tom. 'I'm keeping an eye on him.'

Everyone seemed to be keeping an eye on someone. Einstein was watching Jason, Tom was watching Einstein, and Emma kept looking up at her father. 'Did I mention it was my dad who found the quoll poo?' she asked, over the din.

For his part, Jason kept scanning the crowd to see if David was there. Fortunately, his friend hadn't been seriously injured in the Predator accident; he'd just got a bleeding nose and a knock on the side of the head that had matured into a juicy lump. Jason had had to find that out from David's parents since David wasn't speaking to him. Jason was feeling so guilty that he'd applied for a job at the local Macca's to guarantee he'd have petrol money, just in case David was brave enough to risk another session. Or stupid enough.

But they were nearly at the end of the march, and there was still no sign of David.

Mr Wherrett was there though, and so was the bald guy that everyone said had attacked Sal. He still had a menacing expression on his face but he didn't have his chainsaw with him today, perhaps because the loggers thought they'd already won.

Like last time, as soon as the protesters arrived at the council offices, Gillian addressed the crowd. Today she only talked about quolls, and there was a huge picture of one behind her. The crowd applauded and shouted their agreement. Mr Wherrett was looking down and biting his lower lip.

While Gillian was still speaking, Tom handed his placard to Einstein, then ran over to his van and drove off. Jason was surprised that Gillian's second-in-command didn't hang around until the event was officially over. He nudged Emma and pointed at the departing van. 'He's got to catch a flight to visit his mum,' Emma said. 'She's sick.'

After Gillian had finished, several people in the audience shouted out questions. If a question wasn't quoll-related, the lawyer somehow twisted it until it was. The event was still going strong when a policeman signalled to Gillian that their time was up.

Jason turned to see if Emma wanted any help disassembling the PA system but was interrupted by a tap on the shoulder. 'Jason, you remember me,' said the tapper. 'Marie Torelli, *Sapphire Sentinel*. I was wondering if you had any comment on the PM's withdrawal from the Rotterdam emission control agreement.' She held a recorder of some kind in Jason's face.

Jason wasn't expecting to be accosted by a reporter and couldn't think what to say. After a few embarrassing seconds, he managed to find some words. 'You're not supposed to talk to me, are you? Isn't there a restraining order or something?'

'That doesn't apply here. You've just taken part in a public event to which the media were invited.'

'I don't know….' Jason looked over at Gillian but she was busy with some other reporters.

'You must be very disappointed that Mr Lindsay didn't do what you asked him to do, after you'd saved his life.'

'I don't have any opinions about that any more.'

'Come on Jason, that isn't very news-worthy.'

'I don't want to be news-worthy.' Jason tried to remember how Gillian had dealt with the questions she'd been asked. 'I think the most important thing is saving the quolls.'

'Have you contacted the Prime Minister to let him know how you feel about him turning his back on you?'

Jason desperately wanted to be somewhere else but couldn't work out how to escape. Out of the corner of his eye he saw Emma running across to Gillian.

Even though Jason hadn't answered any of her questions yet, the reporter wouldn't let up. 'Do you regret saving Mr Lindsay's life?'

What a dumb question. Jason didn't know whether he should run away, punch the reporter in the face, or maybe even cry. If this went on much longer, he feared that he'd no longer have a choice and his body would just pick a reaction without his conscious consideration. And that reaction might not be one to be proud of.

Fortunately Gillian intervened and drove Ms Torelli away with the threat of legal action. Jason was shaking; his legs were so weak that he sat down on the ground without meaning to. Gillian helped him up and told Emma to get Tom to talk to the reporters. Emma tried to argue but Gillian shooed her on her way.

'Let's get you some water,' said the lawyer. She guided Jason towards the public toilets at the back of the council building.

Jason was feeling too dizzy to argue. He thought he heard Emma and Einstein arguing behind him and tried to point that out to Gillian, but she was utterly focused on looking after him.

After Jason had had a long drink, Gillian sat him down on a bench and ordered him to stay there for at least ten minutes, then rushed off to see how Tom was coping. Jason was keen to find out too but figured he'd better do what the lawyer had said. It was probably a good idea anyway since he still felt a bit funny and fainting in front of Emma mightn't earn him a lot of respect.

After his timeout had expired, Jason skulked over to the corner of the building and peeped around. The reporters had gone, so he headed over to the remaining greenies. Gillian offered to drop him home but went cold on the idea when Jason mentioned that nobody else would be there. 'I'm not leaving you on your own. Not if you're sick.' Gillian clucked worse than his mother did.

'I'll look after him,' said Emma quickly and surprisingly loudly. 'Only it'll have to be at my house. Because Dad will need help with packing.'

Gillian agreed to that without seeking an opinion from Jason. Not that Jason would have argued; it was a good opportunity to hang out with Emma, even though she was being a bit weird about it.

• • •

Emma's place was specky. The large timber house backed onto the forest and was surrounded by tall gum trees. Tom's van and X-Trail were parked in the circular driveway.

'It's not all ours, sort of,' said Emma. 'Other people stay here for little holidays.' She pointed out a large wooden sign that said 'By Gum Bed and Breakfast Retreat'.

Most of the inside was like a barn, with the kitchen, eating area and lounge room all in one huge space. Everything was clean and fancy and new. Jason had to be careful walking through the place in case he accidentally kicked, elbowed or head-butted any of the billion knick-knacks strewn about.

Judging by the aroma, someone had been cooking. Emma picked up the scent too. She headed for the kitchen and started looking inside the row of large white jars that took up a whole shelf.

Before Emma had tracked down her quarry, Tom burst out of the laundry. 'Oh Emma, I can't seem to find any socks.'

'I told you,' murmured Emma to Jason. 'He's always losing stuff. He reckoned he found more quoll poo last week but now he can't find the bag. It'll probably turn up in the washing machine.'

They went out a side door and Jason looked around the back of the house while Emma took some socks off the clothes line. The yard opened straight out into the forest; a cyclone fence ensured the view was uninterrupted. A wooden deck was adorned with expensive-looking outdoor furniture and a large spa.

'Wow,' said Jason, dipping his hand into the bubbling water.

'I'm not allowed to use it,' said Emma. 'It's only for the guests. Like most things here.'

Emma delivered the socks to Tom, who threw them in his suitcase then rushed out the front door with only a brief 'bye'.

'I wish I was going,' said Jason. 'I love flying.'

Emma screwed up her nose. 'He catches cargo planes owned by the company he works for. They're pretty basic.'

'For free?'

'Uh huh. Which reminds me....' Emma headed back into the kitchen and resumed her examination of the biscuit jars.

'Maybe your mum took the biscuits with her,' suggested Jason.

'She's not my mother,' Emma responded with surprising conviction. 'If they're not here, I know where they'll be.' She extracted her student card from her bag and slid it along the edge of a door labelled 'Waratah Suite'. After a bit of poking, the door clicked open.

The Waratah Suite looked like a hotel room. Clothes were strewn across the bed and suitcases lay open on the floor. Emma tiptoed around the guests' belongings until she reached a bedside table. On it, nestled among various ornaments, was a plate from which she lifted four large biscuits.

'Aren't they for the guests?' asked Jason in a hushed voice.

'They won't miss them.' She passed the biscuits to Jason, who still hadn't entered the room, then went back inside and started rearranging things. She moved the clock from one side of the bed to the other, swapped the positions of some of the pictures and ornaments, and even dragged a lounge chair to the opposite corner of the room.

'Just messing with them,' she explained, in answer to Jason's wide eyes.

'Why?'

'For being here. For invading my place.'

Despite Jason's assurance that four large choc-chip biscuits would be sufficient, Emma proceeded to do the same to the other two guest rooms. She even moved some stuff from one of the rooms to the other.

After she'd finished upsetting the absent guests, the pair sat at the huge carved table that dominated the upper part of the living area. The biscuits were great, although Jason was slowing down by time he got to the end of his quota.

Emma pointed Jason towards the lounge area then disappeared outside. Jason sunk into a leather recliner that faced a massive TV. Behind the TV, floor-to-ceiling windows looked out over the deck to the forest beyond. Occasional raindrops kamikazed onto the glass and slithered downwards. Emma came into view and poured seed into the bird-feeders that were hanging above the deck.

'That's the only thing the dragon lets me do,' she said on her return. 'I can't touch anything else. Well, I'm not supposed to.'

As they watched, a group of eastern rosellas descended on the bird feeders, seemingly oblivious to the gentle precipitation. The rain pattered pleasantly onto the Colorbond roof, and Jason sunk deeper into his chair while Emma provided comments on the birds' antics.

'If I could be bothered getting up, I could take a look at your Dad's computer,' said Jason. 'I wanna see what the loggers' virus looks like.'

'There isn't one.'

'But, Tom said—'

'He keeps reckoning his computer does weird stuff, but he just doesn't know how to use it. I changed the home page in his browser to go to the loggers' site.'

Jason looked incredulous. '*You* did that?'

'Serves him right for being paranoid.'

Five o'clock arrived, and Jason enquired whether it would be okay to turn on the TV to see if the protest march was on the news. Emma went all evasive.

'Won't your mother— the dragon let you watch it?' asked Jason.

'It doesn't work.'

'What about the one in the kitchen?'

Emma didn't respond.

'It's about time I went home anyway,' said Jason. 'I'll catch it there.' He started to pull himself up from the depths of his chair.

'No, don't.'

'Why not?' Jason asked slowly. 'What's going on?'

'You don't want to see it.'

Jason searched his memory of the day's events to try to work out what Emma didn't want him to see. He'd stuffed up the interview with the reporter, but that was nothing new. Anyway, Marie Torelli was a newspaper reporter, not a TV reporter. 'Now I *have* to see it,' he said, and got up to leave.

Emma screwed up her face and clicked the remote control. The TV responded with some footage of the march. Jason looked for himself but he was hidden among the other protesters. 'You can't see me, but that's okay,' he said. 'Is that what you were tense about?'

'No, but maybe it won't be on.'

But it was. Coverage of the march gave way to an interview—with Einstein!

Initially the dimwit stuck to repeating things he'd heard Gillian say, interspersed with the occasional injection of a chant from the march. But then the reporter asked him a question that was a bit trickier: 'Jason Saunders, the teenager who saved the Prime Minister's life, is a member of QAP. What's his role?'

'Oh, Jason's full-on with us,' said Einstein. 'He says the loggers are shit and can rot in hell.'

Jason felt his face turning red. He wanted to shout the truth to the TV, but resisted.

'Is Jason going to ask the PM to intervene?' asked the reporter.

'Deffo, he's gunna do that for us.' Emma could be seen behind Einstein, with a horrified look on her face.

The image panned around to show spectators' reactions. Mr Wherrett, looking out of place in his light grey suit, was writing in a notebook. Where Einstein had had Emma peeping timidly over his shoulder, Mr Wherrett had the big bald chainsaw logger. And the logger didn't seem too happy about what Einstein was saying.

'He's going to kill me,' said Jason in a matter-of-fact voice.

The reporter hadn't finished. 'That car Jason got from the PM. Doesn't it undermine your environmental credentials when your star member creates pollution just for fun?'

'Oh, Jason's not gunna drive it any more. We already told him.'

'I never agreed to that!' blurted Jason.

'I know,' said Emma. 'I tried to stop him but Dad had left and I couldn't find Gillian.'

'It's not your fault,' said Jason, 'but I quit.'

Emma put her hand on Jason's arm. 'Please don't.'

'I have to. If I quit, maybe that guy will only break my legs instead of my neck.'

Chapter 10

Something Fishy

Emma had assured Jason he wouldn't feel so pissed off with the greenies after a good night's sleep. The only problem was that he didn't get a good night's sleep. Whenever he closed his eyes, a vision of the chainsaw logger appeared.

He dragged himself out of bed at 6am wishing he'd quit yesterday when he first thought of it. Since the loggers weren't actually doing any computer hacking, the situation wasn't as interesting as it first seemed. Sure, they shouldn't be killing quolls but his role in stopping that was merely to act as reporter bait, and that wasn't very satisfying.

He forced himself to wait until nine before cycling to Gillian's cabin. Unfortunately, she wasn't there. That was a bummer because he'd wanted to avoid going down to the camping area where most of the greenies were staying. He contemplated calling or texting Gillian but it seemed a bit rude to dump her over the phone.

But there was a good chance Gillian was with the others, and Jason wanted to get this over and done with. Overnight rain had turned the road to mud, so he had to wheel his bike through the park.

Most of the greenies had gathered at the picnic area. Gillian was indeed with them—and she was ripping into Einstein: 'What made you think you could speak to the media on Jason's behalf? What made you think you could speak on the *group's* behalf, for that matter?'

Einstein sat with his head in his hands and spoke uncharacteristically quietly. 'I'm Tom's, you know, second-in-command.'

'Oh really? How do you figure that, Einstein?'

'He gave me his sign.'

Gillian's expression changed from amazement to bewilderment while Jason started imagining all sorts of mystical possibilities, like a secret handshake or glowing eyeballs.

Finally Gillian recovered sufficiently to demand an explanation.

'His sign,' repeated Einstein. 'You know, his banner thing. He gave his to me when he pissed off after the march.'

'Einstein, you are *not* Tom's second-in-command,' said Gillian, looking skyward. 'I don't want you to talk to the media ever again.'

'Okay okay. Just— shhh. My head's killing me.'

The lawyer turned around. Noticing Jason, she beckoned him over. 'Jason, this will never happen again. We're very sorry. Aren't we, Einstein?'

Einstein nodded, without looking up.

'I'm not giving up my Predator,' said Jason.

'Nobody's going to make you,' replied Gillian, 'although it might help—'

Jason shook his head. 'Everyone else is burning fuel, so it won't make any difference whether I do or not. I'm just one person.'

'If you're gunna keep it, at least do something useful with it,' said Einstein. 'We can use it to get to the loggers' place.'

Gillian looked heavenward again. 'I don't want you going anywhere near the loggers' depot again. As long as I'm responsible for what we do, it's going to be legal.' She motioned with her head towards Einstein's haphazardly-parked ute. There was a major dent in the side, and the back end was caked in mud that went as high as the petrol cap.

'The genius tried to pay a visit to our friends in the forest last night,' Gillian explained to Jason. 'Luckily, he didn't make it. We had to tow him out this morning.' She stalked off, shaking her head.

Einstein struggled to his feet and walked slowly to his ute. After getting in, he waved for Jason to come across.

Jason did so, but was careful to stand an arm's length back from the open window.

'If I didn't have a hangover,' said Einstein carefully, 'you and I would be having a little talk.'

'But I didn't do anything!'

Einstein ignored Jason's defence and turned on the radio. The car reverberated with a mixture of screaming and thumping. He groaned and muted the sound, then revved up his damaged vehicle. Jason had to jump backwards to avoid being sprayed with red mud as the ute lurched up the track.

As he pedalled home, Jason tried to make sense of the situation. Both the loggers and the greenies (or at least Einstein) were out to get him, even though he hadn't done anything to incur the wrath of either group. And he'd intended to quit the greenies but somehow hadn't succeeded. At least he'd get to see more of Emma this way—until the loggers or Einstein got to him, anyway.

•　　　•　　　•

After about a week, David had thawed out enough to talk to Jason again. He was still unimpressed with Jason's stunt but was more than happy to exploit the lump on his head by letting selected girls feel it. Jason suggested that David should therefore be grateful to him, but that didn't go over very well.

Unfortunately, Jason's plan to secure a more reliable source of petrol money seemed like it was about to backfire. In a few days time, he had to go to Canberra to receive a bravery award for saving the Prime Minister's life last summer. That meant meeting Mr Lindsay again, which would give the PM the ideal opportunity to ask for his Predator back. Jason could see himself ending up with heaps of petrol but nothing to put it in. He contemplated quitting his job even before he'd started it, but then realised he could save up for a better computer, one that could run the latest *Grand Theft Auto*.

Another threat to the Predator was Jason's parents. They were appalled that his attitude to driving had injured David, and ranted about his performance at school. His mother alternated confusingly between sympathy and anger, while his father simply wanted to withdraw Predator privileges until things improved. Fortunately, Jason was able to appeal to his mother while she was in sympathy mode and managed to avoid any consequences, at least for the time being.

Emma's big news was that Tom had found some more quoll poo during one of his walks in the forest. Unfortunately, he'd left it lying around on the dinner table and the dragon had thrown it out. Emma was livid, but Jason figured the guests probably didn't want to see animal faeces on the dinner table.

Tuesday was Jason's first day on the job at McDonald's. Because he could actually count out change correctly, they put him on the front counter straight away. The register seemed horrifically complicated at first but it wasn't long before he had it sussed.

Just when Jason thought he had everything under control, he noticed Bull in his queue. Fortunately, the thug didn't seem to be up to anything criminal, and just wanted a shake.

'I see you got that sign down okay,' said Jason.

Bull nodded. 'I thought I got sprung when I was dragging it home, but it was only one of them protesters. He reckoned it gave him a brilliant idea. We're gunna do a joint mission sometime.'

That sounded pretty ominous. Fortunately, Bull's shake was ready so Jason didn't get to hear any more details.

Jason's Thursday shift started off quietly. He was wiping the counter when David and a couple of his rugby mates lobbed in.

'I'll just get your garden salad,' said Jason before David had even made it to the counter.

David ignored the jibe. He and his friends strode past the counter and sat down at a table by the window. 'Waiter!' called David, snapping his fingers in the air.

Jason blinked.

'Waiter!' called David again, louder this time.

Jason glared at him, but David had his back to the counter so Jason had to go over to his table.

'Oh, there you are,' said David. 'Menus, please.'

'Don't be a moron. It doesn't work like that and you know it.'

'Oh. Then I'll just have a steak. Medium rare.'

Jason pointed at the menu board.

David studied the menu carefully, even though he and Jason had eaten there hundreds of times. He ordered a burger, changed his mind and ordered nuggets, then swapped back to a burger again.

'I guess there's no chance of you coming over to the counter,' said Jason.

'It's a bit confusing for me,' replied David. 'I've got this bump on the head, see?'

Jason nodded slowly and went off to get David's order.

'And wipe the table,' called David after him. 'There's a speck of sugar on it.'

As Jason was putting his friend's food on a tray, the manager came over and demanded an explanation. Jason assured her that everything was under control.

'Don't forget the salad you got out,' she said.

'Actually, I was just—' Explaining would have taken too long. 'It's for me. I'll eat it later.'

The event was a decisive victory for David. Jason hoped they could put the Predator business behind them now.

During a break, Jason consumed his unwanted salad. Lettuce wasn't really his thing, so he washed it down with two fish burgers even though it was only a couple of hours until tea time. He never wanted to see a piece of fish again.

Just as he was about to get back to work, there was a text from Gillian:

> *Dinner @ Hendrick's @ 6pm. The fish & chips r on me. Don't b late!!*

●   ●   ●

Hendrick's Seafood Restaurant was only a couple of blocks from McDonalds, but Jason figured they wouldn't let him in if he was wearing his McDonald's uniform so he had to rush home and change.

When he arrived at the restaurant, he was shown to a private dining room upstairs. Most of the greenies, or QAPers as Emma called them, were already there. Even Einstein was wearing a coat and tie, which looked totally wrong. On the other hand, Emma, in a purple dress, looked great but Jason couldn't bring himself to say so.

Nobody seemed to know what had prompted Gillian's sudden fit of generosity, and Gillian herself hadn't arrived yet. It was also strange that the invitations had said to be there by six even though the buffet didn't start until half an hour later. Maybe the lawyer had stuffed up.

A side door flew open and two men wheeled in a trolley with a TV on it. Gillian was with them, and motioned for them to hurry up. After some frantic plugging and button-pushing, the six o'clock news came on but with the volume turned down low. Everyone watched in silence as a couple of presumably irrelevant stories came and went. Then Gillian turned up the volume.

> *After discussions with the government, the company responsible for logging operations in Sapphire State Forest has agreed to suspend its operations pending further—*

Chaos erupted. Whoops and applause, hand-shaking and even hugging. The din went on for so long that one of the restaurant staff burst into the room and gave Gillian a dirty look.

Order was restored just as Mr Wherrett appeared on the TV. Some of the greenies booed, and one of them threw something at the screen. Gillian held up her hand for silence so they could hear what the logger said.

> *I'd like to point out that we're doing this voluntarily. We're an environmentally-responsible company and we absolutely won't be harming any endangered species. However, the evidence for quolls in Sapphire Forest is inconclusive, and we're commencing an investigation into the matter immediately. We're confident that we'll be able to resume our restoration of the forest in the near future.*

Nobody seemed to take Mr Wherrett's comments seriously, and when the food arrived, the greenies got stuck into it like it was Christmas. Jason was still full of fish burger so the mountains of seafood had absolutely no appeal to him. However, he took great pleasure in peeling prawns for Emma and popping them into her mouth.

'How come the loggers reckon there's no evidence of quolls?' Jason asked.

Emma shrugged as she chewed.

Tom had found quoll poo, hadn't he? Jason had even held it in his hands. Maybe the loggers knew something about it that the greenies didn't.

Chapter 11

A Log of Grievances

At least the bravery award ceremony meant a day off school and a plane flight to Canberra. Other than that, there wasn't much to look forward to. Even if Mr Lindsay didn't demand his car back from Jason, it was bound to be embarrassing for both of them since the PM had wimped out of the emission control agreement. Jason couldn't get his head around being treated like a hero and worthless at the same time.

Fortunately it wasn't up to Mr Lindsay to hand out the bravery award. That was going to be done by someone called Mr Riddell, who was the Governor-General. Jason's dad had explained that the Governor-General was sort-of in charge of all of the politicians, including Mr Lindsay.

After flying into Canberra airport, Jason and his parents were driven to Government House, which was where the Governor-General lived. The place looked more like an old hotel; it was three storeys high and creamy white.

The family was escorted to a large room that was empty except for some old furniture around the edges. About twenty people were standing around talking. Jason recognised some of his relatives, and Chris from the Sapphire Bay Surf Lifesaving Club was there too. They all shook Jason's hand and congratulated him as though he'd just finished saving the PM when it was actually months ago.

Unfortunately, several TV crews and reporters were also present. They were hovering around the perimeter of the room like vultures. Jason tried to hide among the guests even though he realised the reporters knew full well he was there. After all, he was the reason they were there.

Mr Riddell arrived a few minutes before the ceremony was supposed to start. Jason's parents got all flustered and didn't know what to say to him, but Jason thought the Governor-General just seemed like a normal person, except for his brilliant silver hair.

Not surprisingly, the PM arrived late. As soon as he rushed in, everyone was called to silence and Mr Riddell launched into a speech. It was obviously a talk he'd given heaps of times before since he didn't have any notes and he didn't refer to Jason once. He just went on about the value of bravery, the importance of youth, yada yada yada.

Jason looked out the window. The grounds seemed like a golf course, with lush green grass stretching off into the distance. Four kangaroos hopped out from behind a clump of trees and stopped in the middle of the lawn. Jason nudged his mother and pointed out the window, but she redirected his attention back to the speech.

Finally Mr Riddell started to talk about Jason. He picked up a framed certificate and read out a description of what happened on the evening of the rescue—although, if Jason hadn't known it was supposed to be about that event, he mightn't have recognised it since the certificate made it sound much more impressive than it actually was.

That wasn't the only problem with Mr Riddell's speech. He said Jason was an excellent student who always wanted what's best for others. He wouldn't have said that if he'd heard about Jason's recent performance. It would certainly have been relevant since saving Mr Lindsay had given the PM the opportunity to show Jason that he was stupid and irrelevant.

The Governor-General called Jason to come out the front with him, then read the final line from the certificate: 'For outstanding courage and selflessness, I hereby award you the Commendation for Brave Conduct.' He pinned a medal on Jason's coat, handed him the certificate, then shook his hand. The reporters went mad with their mega flashes while everyone else applauded. Jason turned red and tugged on the medal's ribbon as though tempting it to come off.

Finally the embarrassment was over, save for everyone wanting to congratulate Jason again and inspect his trinkets. Jason was more interested in the stream of waiters bringing out platters of little pies and sausage rolls, sandwiches and miscellaneous things on biscuits. He waited for the big-wigs to hook in, but the Governor-General said 'you're the VIP today' and motioned for him to go first.

Jason loaded a plate with hot food. It was like a birthday party, except that everything was up-market. Jason's father wasn't impressed, though: he sampled a biscuit with raw salmon on it and crinkled up his nose. 'My salmon's better,' he said.

The waiters started handing out coffee cups, then came around with fancy silver teapots. They didn't ask Jason what he wanted, but presented him with a large cold glass. It was a chocolate thickshake! How did they know? Jason looked over to Mr Lindsay. Noticing Jason's gaze, the PM winked while holding up his coffee cup in a 'cheers' motion.

To Jason's surprise, the reporters left him alone, although they still took the occasional photo. Jason gave them plenty of opportunities to collect images of him testing out the sausage rolls, which were especially tasty.

Unfortunately, while distracted with the food table, Jason failed to keep an eye on his mother. After scanning the crowd, his fears were confirmed: she was in deep discussion with Mr Lindsay in a corner of the room. Mrs Saunders was doing all the talking, while the PM frowned and looked floorwards. Jason could feel his ears burning. The sausage rolls didn't taste quite as good after that.

Not long later, Jason turned in response to a tap on the shoulder.

'I hope you're looking after the Predator,' said Mr Lindsay.

This is where he asks for it back, thought Jason. Mrs Saunders must have mentioned the accident to him.

'Well, at least I won't need to work for petrol money any more,' said Jason.

Mr Lindsay looked confused.

The PM's confusion confused Jason. 'You're taking it back, aren't you?'

'Why would I do that? It's your reward. You saved my life, remember?' The PM tapped the frame in Jason's hand. 'It says so right there.'

Several reporters were creeping closer. Jason eyed them warily.

'Guys, not today, remember?' Mr Lindsay said to them, causing them to scuttle away like a bunch of exposed cockroaches.

The PM led Jason into a small adjoining room. 'Your mother thought you might want to talk about the Rotterdam withdrawal.'

'No, it's none of my business.'

'That doesn't sound like the young man who gave me such a hard time last summer.'

'It's not. He's gone. I've learnt my lesson.'

The PM looked at Jason thoughtfully. 'You know that other countries are going to emit heaps of greenhouse gases whether Australia does or not?'

Jason nodded.

'So it doesn't make much difference what Australia does?'

Jason nodded again.

Despite being agreed with, the PM looked displeased. 'I'm not sure you understand.'

'I understand very well.'

A man in a dark suit stuck his head into the room and knocked quietly on the door frame. When he'd got Mr Lindsay's attention, he tapped his watch.

The PM frowned. 'I'm worried about you, Jason. I've heard you're not doing too well.'

Jason stared at the parquetry on the coffee table in front of him. The man at the door tapped his watch again.

'Okay, okay,' said Mr Lindsay. 'Jason, I've got to go, but you know you can call me at any time if you want to talk.'

Jason nodded once more as the PM swept out of the room.

•   •   •

It had been a long day. Jason sat on his bed at home and studied his certificate. Everyone said the ceremony was a great honour, but it just left Jason feeling bad because of the nice things they said about him that were no longer true. 'Commendation for Brave Conduct,' he read from the box of his medal. He wasn't even brave enough to make a decision any more. He tossed the medal and certificate into the bottom drawer of his desk and went to bed.

•   •   •

Jason was woken by the roar of an engine outside. It sounded like a model aeroplane, but the bedside clock said 2:47am so that seemed unlikely.

The engine revved a few times, which enabled Jason to identify it. It wasn't a model aeroplane; it was a chainsaw!

Memories tumbled through Jason's head. There was the bald logger hacking away with his saw during the first protest march, Sal's mysterious fate, Einstein making Jason look bad on TV, and the bald logger's furious reaction.

The revving gave way to the buzz of wood being cut. Jason scrunched up in bed with eyes wide, although there was nothing to see. His hands gripped the top of his doona so tightly they hurt.

The saw finished its cut and fell silent. Jason listened hard to try to work out what was happening. The sound of the saw was still ringing in his ears, but it seemed to be silent. Hopefully that was the end of it.

It wasn't. The bedroom window shattered and the venetian blinds clattered. Something thudded to the floor on the far side of the room.

Jason caught himself just before he wet the bed.

Before the venetians had stopped jangling, Mr Saunders burst into the room and flicked on the light. 'What the hell…?'

Jason couldn't manage any words.

'Are you okay?' asked his father as he scanned the room.

'Yes.'

'Right.' Mr Saunders rushed out of the room as quickly as he'd arrived. Jason heard him go outside. 'Who's there?' he called a couple of times.

Jason sat up and put his feet on the floor after checking there was no glass in the vicinity. His attempt to stand was unsuccessful because his legs were shaking and had no strength. *Another triumph for the bravery award winner*, he thought. Maybe he could send his medal back to Mr Riddell so it could be given to someone who deserved it.

From his vantage point on the floor, Jason looked around the room. Unsurprisingly, a log was lying near the door. Actually, it was half a log. A message was written on the flat face: 'BUTT OUT U LITTLE ARSEHOLE ELSE NEXT 1 WILL BE ON FIRE'.

•   •   •

Nobody said much at breakfast. Jason hadn't had much sleep and his parents didn't look like they'd fared any better. Not that there'd been much opportunity; by the time the cops left, it was almost 4am.

Mr Saunders was still livid and wanted to go straight down to the loggers' depot and 'return their log'. Jason pointed out that the family car wouldn't be able to handle the rough track and jokingly offered to drive his father there in his Predator, but his father wasn't in the mood for jokes. Mrs Saunders put an end to any such plans by pointing out that they didn't have any proof the loggers were responsible for the deed.

The log had been placed on the kitchen table for the police to examine last night. It was still there at breakfast time, now flanked by the margarine and the Vegemite. It was a surreal image. Jason grabbed a picture of it with his phone.

'I'm not going to be haunted by that thing any more,' Jason's father said tersely. ' "Next one will be on fire", will it? Top idea; let's put this gift to good use.' He strode into the lounge room with the log and flung it into the fireplace. A shower of glowing embers sprayed out.

'That wasn't very bright,' said Jason's mother. 'The police could have used that for evidence.'

Mr Saunders grunted. 'Can't get fingerprints off a log.'

Watching the nocturnal missile burn was surprisingly satisfying. Light from the flames highlighted the texture of the sawn surface: an irregular pattern of lines at two distinct angles, which showed where the logger had changed the direction of his cutting. Jason retrieved his corn flakes from the kitchen and finished them in front of the fire. By the time he had to leave for school, the writing had burnt off the log and it had fallen in among the others.

• • •

'Impressive,' said Bull, idly chiselling away at the surface of his desk. 'You'll wanna come with us tomorrow night, then.'

'Where?' asked Jason suspiciously.

'Loggers' sign.'

Jason looked down. 'I think I've had enough of taking sides.'

'You can't just let 'em win! Some of your greenie mates will be there.'

That seemed doubtful since the greenies thought they'd already beaten the loggers. Unfortunately, the teacher strode in before Jason could get more info.

• • •

Jason caught up with Emma at lunch time to see if Bull was telling the truth. Emma hadn't heard about last night's incident; when Jason told her, she went all clucky and even squeezed his hand. That seemed out of character for the wanna-be Goth but Jason didn't complain.

'Have you heard our news?' asked Emma.

Jason figured she was probably talking about the mission Bull had mentioned, but just in case she meant something else he shook his head. Emma stuffed around with her phone for a while, then handed it over. Jason read the web page she'd called up:

According to the initial analysis, the droppings found in the Sapphire State Forest are not necessarily those of the eastern quoll. The sample was contaminated with

DNA from multiple sources, including human. Florian Wherrett, Australian Forestry Industries' site manager, welcomed the news: 'While it's sad that quolls are almost certainly extinct here, at least we can make the most of what we've got. We hope to resume operations to restore the forest very soon.'

'Maybe I shouldn't have dumped that stuff on your hands,' said Emma.

'Would've been fine with me,' replied Jason, instinctively wiping his hands on his trousers. 'So the greenies— um, QAPers, are going to do something?'

'Gillian said this has made us look like idiots, so of course. And after what the loggers just did to you, double of course.'

•　　•　　•

Jason's parents conveniently assumed he was going to David's after dinner on Friday, so he didn't have to lie to them. He just didn't correct them.

He cycled towards the forest without knowing quite what was going down. He wasn't even sure why he was going, for that matter. Obviously having a log heaved through his bedroom window was part of it, and the fact that Emma was going to be there was another part of it. On the other hand, the loggers could have been right all along about the poo sample. Maybe it wasn't from a quoll. If they weren't lying, it didn't seem right to get back at them or try to stop them fixing the forest.

Jason dismounted at the start of the slushy track that lead to the loggers' depot. About ten silhouettes were there, including Bull and his thuggy mates, and Einstein and his drinking buddies. The fading twilight made it hard to work out who the others were.

Einstein noticed Jason looking around the group and shone a torch straight into his face. 'Your girlfriend isn't here,' he said bluntly.

'She's not my girlfriend,' replied Jason, although he wasn't sure what the situation actually was in that regard. 'Is Tom here?'

'That wuss? Tasmania.'

'Thank God,' added a voice from the shadows.

This didn't feel right. Jason wanted to get back on his bike and speed home, but he didn't dare.

'You sure we can't get in there?' asked someone, flashing a beam of light up the track into the forest.

'Nope,' said Einstein. 'Tried it.'

'Okay, we'll just do the sign.' A bag was unzipped and tools rattled.

'Youse'll need this too,' said Einstein, and started tossing cans of beer to the others. One sailed in Jason's direction but the torchlight moved away at the last moment so he fluffed the catch. The cold projectile hit him on the side of the head. A can was opened beside him, spraying him with a mist that smelt like rotting vegetables. Jason put his can aside.

The sign was larger than it seemed from the road. It was taller than Jason, and looked heavy. A lot of swearing was emanating from the men wielding the spanners at its base because they couldn't budge the bolts holding the sign to its concrete footings. Jason didn't mind that at all; hopefully they'd have to give up and go home.

'You lot are lucky I came prepared,' said Bull. Jason recognised the *clack clack clack* of a can of spray paint being shaken.

Einstein nodded. 'Yeah, okay. It's better than nothin'.'

'Saunders, get here and make yourself useful,' ordered Bull. He made Jason kneel on the soggy ground, then climbed onto his back.

'You wouldn't like to take your boots off, would you?' asked Jason.

'Nope.'

A couple of Einstein's mates illuminated the sign while Bull blasted away. Jason copped a fair bit of overspray and tried to spit the taste of it out of his mouth, which made Einstein laugh.

'Car!' said one of the torch-bearers. They killed their torches and scrambled into the bush. Bull jumped off his makeshift pedestal, causing Jason to topple onto the muddy road.

Shadows swirled around them as the car's headlights diffused through the gums. They lay in the undergrowth until the car was well past the forest turnoff.

The torches switched on again, and Bull got back up on Jason and resumed work. By now, Jason had learnt to keep his eyes and mouth tightly closed.

'Good job,' said Einstein after a few minutes. Bull jumped down and Jason was careful to keep his balance this time.

Jason tried to see what Bull had done to the sign but the torches were now illuminating the way to the cars. Einstein and his mates threw their empty cans into the bush and jumped into their vehicles, taking Bull and his crew with them. The cars fishtailed down the track before sliding onto the asphalt and leaving Jason alone in the darkness. Nobody had even bothered to say goodbye.

Jason stared at the receding tail lights, mouth agape, breathing smoke in the cold air. After the cars had disappeared, he groped his way to his bike and headed home. His muddy bum slipped around on the bike seat, warning him to clean himself up a bit before reaching his destination. But he'd had enough and just wanted to climb into bed.

So this was revenge. He'd now paid back the loggers for their contribution to the Saunders family's stock of firewood. Surely revenge should have felt better than this. As it was, the experience was so unpleasant that it seemed more like another victory for the loggers.

At least it would take them ages to get their sign clean.

Chapter 12

Thinners and Thinning

Jason scrubbed at the sign, squirted more solvent on it, and scrubbed again. This was no way to spend a Sunday morning. His arms ached, his shoulders ached and his neck ached.

Below him, Bull sat with his back against one of the sign's legs and puffed on a cigarette. 'I should probably slug you for vandalising my artwork.'

'You could always clean it off yourself,' suggested Jason.

'Nah, I'm not that destructive.'

The bits up high were the hardest. Jason tried jumping and standing on his toes, but neither tactic was very effective. The obvious solution was to stand on Bull, like Bull had stood on him on Friday night, but that would have resulted in more pain than he was already in.

'So how did they catch you?' asked Jason.

'At first I thought you dobbed me in, 'cause my mum knew. You know she works for your dad.'

Jason didn't know that, but it didn't make any difference. 'I never told anyone!'

Bull nodded and kicked at the vinyl gym bag beside him. 'I left this here. Loggers found it.'

'Silly boy.'

'Hey, you're here too.'

Jason grunted. He should have listened to the alarm bells in his head before rushing home on Friday. His parents had sprung him smelling of alcohol and with paint in his hair, even though it was only overspray in both cases. He fessed up to his part in the crime, hoping his father's agreement that the logging should be stopped might count in his favour.

It didn't. His parents were furious. Jason didn't try to argue against their deluge. For a start, he was too tired; secondly, it wouldn't have been wise to interrupt. Mostly, though, he knew they were right. When Emma said QAP was going to do something, he had no idea she meant damaging other people's property. She might have had a habit of messing with the guests at her parents' house, but it was still a surprise that she was into stuff like this. Not that she'd bothered to show up in person.

Tyres screeching on the main road made Jason look around. Einstein's ute turned from the asphalt and bounced along the dirt before skidding to a halt a few centimetres short of the sign—right where Jason had been standing before he took refuge behind one of its supports.

One of Einstein's moronic friends leaned out the passenger's window and pointed at the sign. 'You missed a spot.'

'Up yours,' replied Bull without looking up.

Jason looked across at Einstein. 'Nobody suspects you?'

'No paint on me. Why do you reckon I let youse guys do the dirty work?' He tapped the side of his head. 'That's why they call me Einstein.'

Jason decided against correcting him. The genius wouldn't understand the subtlety of sarcasm.

Einstein did an ugly U-turn and pulled up beside Jason again. 'Just make sure nobody starts to suspect,' he said, then took off emitting jets of mud from his rear tyres.

Jason watched the ute skid around a corner, ignoring the stop sign. How come Einstein was allowed to drive on the road, and he wasn't? He could drive much more safely than Einstein when he wanted to. It just seemed like discrimination. He was trapped in the rut of McKenzie's field and the make-believe of computer games just because he hadn't had enough birthdays.

He resumed work on the sign, and Bull lit another cigarette. It was impossible to get rid of the graffiti without also damaging the original paint. The loggers would probably have to get the whole thing redone, so removing the graffiti wasn't particularly helpful. But Jason knew the main reason they were there was to be punished—even though only he, a mere accomplice, was actually doing any work.

Another car approached, this time coming out of the forest. The drab green Range Rover pulled up sedately, and Mr Wherrett and the chainsaw logger got out.

Mr Wherrett looked down at Bull, who hadn't bothered to get up. 'And what are you doing, Charles?'

'Taking a break,' replied Bull, hiding his cigarette beside him. 'And don't call me Charles.'

'I'm surprised at you, Jason,' said Mr Wherrett. 'I saw you on TV with the PM, getting that award. What would Graham Lindsay say about this?'

'He'd say it doesn't make any difference whether I did it or not, because the others were going to do it anyway.'

The bald logger made a move towards Jason but Mr Wherrett pulled him back.

'Isn't this all a bit silly?' said Mr Wherrett. 'You mouth off about us on TV, someone throws a log through your window—and it wasn't us—then you vandalise our property, so we punish you. When's it all going to end?'

'I never said those things on TV!'

'And we didn't chuck that log,' said the chainsaw logger in a gravelly voice. 'Get a clue.'

'Shut up, Roscoe,' snapped Mr Wherrett, before turning back to Jason. 'What matters is that people *believe* you said those things. People take them seriously because of your reputation. You need to be careful—'

Mr Wherrett's phone rang, and he excused himself and walked back to his car to take the call. Roscoe followed, so Jason shot a few blasts of solvent at the graffiti and rubbed away at it.

Bull continued to relax and made up for lost time with his cigarette. The smoke drifted into Jason's nostrils. He'd been hit with overspray from beer cans and spray paint, and now this. After plucking up the courage to glare at Bull, he noticed drips of solvent falling from the bottom of the sign onto Bull's gym bag. A few extra squirts from the solvent bottle increased the flow nicely. Jason figured there was a good chance the solvent would eat holes through the vinyl, or at least leave blotches. Two could play the overspray game, and it served Bull right for not helping.

Jason heard the loggers coming back and got scrubbing again. 'Now, where were we?' said Mr Wherrett. 'Oh yes. When's this game going to end?'

Jason thought for a while. 'When you give up, or when you've cut down the forest.'

'We have no intention of cutting down the forest. We're just thinning it, for its own good.'

Jason had always assumed that thinning was just the loggers' word for cutting down trees. Mr Wherrett seemed to be implying something more subtle.

The logger detected Jason's uncertainty. 'Things aren't always as they seem, are they? Are you sure you're on the right side?'

'Why do I have to be on a side?' murmured Jason, not really wanting an answer.

'There's a lot of science behind ecological thinning. Even maths. You'd probably find it interesting.'

'Sounds like bullshit to me,' said Bull, eliciting a glare from Roscoe.

'There's no hope for you, Mr Saint Michael,' replied Mr Wherrett. 'But Jason's smart enough to think about it.' He pivoted on his dress shoes and strode back to his car with Roscoe at his heels, then drove off.

It took hours to get the sign clean. Bull actually contributed from time to time, but not enough to make Jason feel guilty about dripping solvent onto his bag. Mr Wherrett reappeared about lunch time to inspect their work, then let the two vandals head home.

•　　•　　•

Jason got himself a sandwich for lunch. He retreated into his room to eat it, thus avoiding his parents who were probably still in lecture mode.

Mr Wherrett's words about thinning kept rattling around inside his head. Maybe there was more to it than the greenies thought. After all, there were two sides to every argument. Jason had learnt that lesson the hard way, from fighting the PM over emission control targets.

He woke up his computer and googled 'ecological thinning' even though he expected to find basically nothing, like when he'd tried 'logical thinning'.[1]

But this time there were squillions of pages. Some were long and complicated, with statistics and graphs; others were official-looking, from government departments. Jason downloaded some of the more promising pages just in case they disappeared in future.

The basic idea seemed to be that some forests might be healthier if some of their trees were removed. If the trees grow too close to one another, they interfere with each other so none of them does very well. The trees also affect the other plants and animals. Even global warming could come into it, since rising temperatures might mean that forests need to be less dense to survive properly.

One link lead to another, and Jason soon found some equations that claimed to show how a forest grew—or deteriorated. To use them, you had to know a lot of things about the trees, soil and weather. That made sense. What was weird, though, was that the equations seemed to depend on themselves: if you tell them the number of trees at the start, they'd tell you how many trees there'd be next year. Then if you put that number back into the equations, they'd tell you how many trees there'd be the year after.

You had to keep going around in circles. That seemed like a dumb way to work things out.[2]

To make sure he wasn't missing anything, Jason decided to try the equations out. The web site didn't provide all the numbers the equations needed, so he had to use some guesses. It took about five minutes of calculator work to crunch through the equations. Finally, the calculator told him that if you started with 1,000 trees, next year you'd have 1,002.7 trees. Not much different.

Jason went around again, this time starting with 1,002.7. Most of the other numbers were the same as before so it was annoying to have to punch them in again. After another five minutes of tedious button-pushing, the calculator reckoned there'd be -7,462,803.9 trees. That didn't seem very likely.

Figuring he'd made a mistake, Jason tried again. This time, he got 1003.6. That seemed more reasonable, but still wasn't very different from the 1,000 he started with. Forests obviously took a long time to do anything interesting.

But the equations also took a long time, especially considering you'd need dozens of years of results before you could see what was really happening. And then you'd have to do it all again with different numbers to see if thinning made things better or worse. It just wasn't a realistic thing to do. Not with just a calculator, anyway.

'Jason, visitor,' called his mother from the front door. She still sounded a bit pooey.

Emma pushed Jason's bedroom door open and gazed around the room.

Jason hoped the table of numbers he'd scrawled down didn't indicate what he'd been working on. Then he realised his computer was still showing a web page titled 'Ecological Thinning: The Benefits'. He leaned over and casually turned off the monitor, hoping the action didn't seem suspicious.

'I heard about the sign,' said Emma, without making eye contact.

'You *heard* about it? You're the one who told me to do it!'

Emma looked up in surprise. 'I never!'

'You said you were going to do something because the loggers said the quoll poo wasn't quoll poo.'

'Yes, but not *that,*' replied Emma, blinking. 'I didn't even know about it. Do you think Gillian would let anyone in QAP do that?'

'What about Ein—' Jason caught himself just in time, or so he hoped.

Emma slanted her head. 'What about … Einstein?'

'No, what about, um, ironing out what you meant when you said QAP was going to do something?'

Emma still looked suspicious but answered the question. 'We're all going looking for quolls in the forest. Next weekend.'

'So I got into trouble for nothing,' said Jason, flopping back on his chair.

Chapter 13

Jason Puts His Foot in It

Another week of school oozed by. Everyone was surprised when they heard that Jason was involved in the graffiti attack. David didn't approve, but the tougher students thought it was excellent—except for the getting caught bit.

The quoll search was shaping up to be a major event. Ever since the quoll droppings had supposedly been found, the story had been in the national news. Mr Wherrett had been on some current affairs show and announced that he'd give $1,000 to anyone who could find evidence of eastern quolls in the forest. He said it was because he was concerned and didn't want to harm any rare wildlife, but Emma reckoned he was just trying to make himself seem like a good guy.

Whatever, $1,000 would just about buy a new computer that could hack the latest *Grand Theft Auto*. But not quite. Last year, Jason's parents might have been be willing to make up the difference, but given his current behaviour and school performance, that was even less likely than finding poo from an extinct animal.

Saturday was cool and cloudy. Jason propped his bike against a tree near the main entrance to the forest. The parking area was overflowing, with cars parked into the distance in every direction. The quoll search had a bigger turnout than Sapphire Bay's annual street carnival, even though the best entertainment anyone could hope for was to pick up animal droppings. That didn't reflect favourably on the street carnival at all.

Jason spotted Tom's greying mess of hair poking out above the crowd in the picnic area. Unfortunately, Einstein was with him. But Emma was there too, so Jason went over.

'You know this is all your fault, don't you?' greeted Einstein.

'Huh?'

'You're the one who buggered up the shit Tom found.'

Jason was about to defend himself but that would have meant incriminating Emma, so he just said 'Oh'.

Gillian tapped Jason on the shoulder, then beckoned him away from the others. Jason looked down. He knew what the lawyer was going to say but figured he'd better let her say it anyway.

'I know you were only getting revenge for what the loggers did, but we mustn't bring ourselves down to their level. If we get a bad reputation, we might was well go home. Get me some evidence about who threw the log and I'll have them in court so fast that their head will spin.'

Jason nodded and promised to tell her if any evidence cropped up.

Gillian looked at her watch, then stepped onto one of the picnic tables. After holding up an arm to get attention, she thanked everyone for coming then got Tom to tell them what they were looking for. Plastic bags were distributed while Tom spoke. Finally, Gillian declared the event officially under way.

People started meandering into the forest in random directions. Most of them seemed to be treating it as a social activity; nobody seemed to be actually looking for anything. School emu parades were better organised than this.

Jason wanted to bolt ahead of the pack, but Tom and Einstein just stood where they were and kept yacking. When the picnic area was almost empty, Jason couldn't hide his impatience any longer. 'Aren't we going to go?' he asked.

'Isn't a race,' replied Tom. 'Would suit me if someone else found the evidence this time, anyway.'

You're not hanging out for a new computer, thought Jason. He contemplated heading off on his own, but obviously Tom knew what he was looking for since he'd found the stuff before, maybe twice. It made sense to stick close to him. Plus, it was pretty safe to assume Emma wouldn't stray far from his side.

After Einstein and his mates departed, Tom, Emma and Jason were the only ones left. Tom surveyed the search parties as they dissipated into the shadows, then frowned. 'Nobody's going the right way,' he murmured.

'Then let's go the right way ourselves,' said Jason.

'Guess we'll have to. I've always got lucky just doing my regular route.'

They trudged off towards Mount Gore, whose rocky peak was visible through the trees. Jason walked a few metres to Tom's left so he wouldn't be seeing exactly the same bit of ground. Emma did likewise on the other side.

Staring continually at the forest floor made the walk pretty boring. Jason glanced across at Emma and saw she was having a problem with it too. The calls from cockatoos and rosellas kept pulling her attention up into the tree canopy. Her father noticed her misdirected focus and remarked that quolls weren't known for their flying ability.

Tom walked surprisingly quickly but stopped every now and then to poke at the ground with a stick. Jason would have found a stick for himself but he didn't want to get into trouble for not concentrating on the ground. It seemed somehow wrong to be walking through the bush without being allowed to look at the trees since the trees were the whole reason they were doing this.

They went over a crest and interrupted a mob of kangaroos. The animals eyed the walkers suspiciously, then hopped away when the trio got too close. Emma said it was sort-of unfortunate that kangaroos weren't endangered in the forest because evidence of their presence was all over the place.

After they'd been hiking for about fifteen minutes, Tom stopped again. 'See here?' he said, poking at the dirt with his stick. 'Animal trail.'

Emma came across and inspected the grooves. 'Quolls?'

'You never know.' Tom pointed along the ground with his stick, stopping at a spot in front of Jason.

Jason couldn't see anything. Maybe there was a slight channel in the ground, or maybe Tom just had an over-active imagination.

'Can't see it?' asked Tom.

Jason shook his head, and walked closer to where Tom was pointing.

'Back up,' said Tom. 'You've gone past it.'

Jason turned around and stepped slowly. The forest floor was littered with leaves, which he sifted with his right boot.

Tom and Emma watched closely. Tom motioned for Jason to move to his left.

Jason did so, even though there seemed to be no good reason to go that direction. He nudged a few more leaves off the ground in front of him, while Tom stood rigidly and stared from a few metres away.

'Yuck,' said Jason, screwing up his nose at the slime that had accumulated on his boot. He wiped it against a bush.

'What are you doing?' asked Tom shrilly.

'Getting crap off my boot.'

'Why?'

Jason stopped wiping and looked over. Surely the man was kidding. But Tom was still staring back, his eyes even wider than before. Jason had to pick his words carefully so as not to sound sarcastic. 'Who wants mud on their boots?'

'Maybe that isn't mud.'

Jason looked down. 'You mean it *is* crap?' Instinctively he resumed wiping his boot but was interrupted by a shriek from Emma.

Father and daughter came over to assess the damage. Tom did a bit of careful leaf excavation with his stick before declaring that Jason had only winged the sample.

'Is it quoll?' asked Emma.

Tom rolled the remains of the deposit into a Ziploc bag, which he then held up and examined. 'Looks like the other samples,' he declared.

'We could get Jason to see if it *feels* the same,' said Emma.

Jason responded with a wrinkled nose and shaken head.

After Jason had finished cleaning his boot, Tom handed him the sample and told him to be careful with it. 'A lot of people's incomes depend on that stuff.'

—not to mention a new computer for me, thought Jason as he rolled up the bag and placed it in his top pocket. When he looked up, he was surprised to see Tom and Emma heading back the way they'd come. 'Shouldn't we keep looking, in case this isn't from a quoll?' he asked.

Tom stopped and turned, with a surprised expression on his face. 'Your right, of course.'

The track got steeper as they approached Mount Gore. Jason examined a few more animal trails, now using a stick to do the dirty work. A couple of times he came across more droppings but Tom quickly dismissed them as kangaroo.

After they'd been going for about an hour, they turned around. Jason wanted to return via a different route so they could look for evidence of quolls in other places. Emma was up for it even though she was tired from going uphill, but Tom said they should stick to the track.

Jason still kept a lookout for animal trails on the way back. Now that he knew what he was looking for, he spotted some he hadn't seen before. Unfortunately, it was pretty hard to get Tom to stop so he could check them out.

They smelt the barbecues before they could see them. It was about mid-day when they got back to the picnic area, and most of the other searchers were already there.

'Here's the man,' said Gillian. 'Jackpot again, Tom?'

Jason proudly held up his plastic bag. 'Tom struck out. I didn't, though!'

Gillian took the bag and studied its contents. 'That's definitely worth testing. I hope this lot is clean.'

'He got it all over his foot this time,' said Emma.

Gillian, who was lowering the bag into a small esky, looked up in horror. Einstein uttered a profanity.

'I did not!' protested Jason. 'I never touched this bit.'

'Let's hope not,' said the lawyer.

Chapter 14

Calculated Risks

Waiting for the results of the latest quoll sample test was painful. It was bad enough last time, but this time Jason had $1,000 riding on the outcome.

Compared to the battle over the forest, nothing at school seemed real. Fortunately there were only a few days left before school holidays. Jason was wasting time at a computer in the library when David rocked up.

'Hey Jase, wanna help me with spreadsheets sometime?'[3]

'Spread … what?'

'Chandra crapped on about them in IT. I didn't get it. Only 'cause of his accent, you understand.'

David brought up the spreadsheet program on the computer Jason was using and started firing questions at him.

Jason studied the screen then pressed a few keys, accidentally overwriting the equation David had been trying to enter.

'Looks like I'll have to read the handouts,' lamented David. 'Coming to maths?'

Jason shook his head and kept fiddling with the computer.

'Maybe you should,' said David as he walked out.

Jason kept tinkering with the spreadsheet. It wasn't like anything he'd seen before. It seemed to be able to do lots of calculations at the same time, which was pretty clever. The hard part was working out how to tell it what calculations to do. Jason tried entering a few equations but the program kept complaining about a 'circular reference'. That was dumb because Jason had never referred to a circle.[4]

After about an hour, Jason had to admit defeat. The spreadsheet was just too weird, which was a shame because it could probably have chewed through the forest thinning equations in a second.

• • •

'Einstein wants to talk to you,' said Emma, after Wednesday's English class.

'Hasn't he worked out how to use his phone yet?'

'He wants to talk in person. To apologise, or something.'

'Then he can drive over,' said Jason.

'His car's being repaired. He dinged it in the forest.'

That was plausible.

After school, Jason cycled down to the caravan park, hoping Einstein wasn't going to be there—even though the half-wit definitely owed him an apology for leaving him to cop the heat for the sign job. The incident had made it into the local paper, but it had been quickly overshadowed by the latest quoll poo finding.

Unfortunately, Einstein was there. Despite the cold weather, his caravan was like an oven. Pizza debris decorated Einstein's singlet, although judging by the smell, it might not have been from today.

The rugby on TV was so loud it was hard to hear what Einstein was saying. The wave of his beer can presumably meant 'sit down', so Jason used an empty pizza box to push the dirty clothes from a spot on the lounge, and sat.

Einstein didn't seem to be in any hurry to apologise. He focused on the TV and swore at the referee when a try was disallowed, then muted the sound in disgust.

'Remember your bedroom window?' he said, turning to face Jason. 'Since you cleaned the sign, it's like we never got back at them bastards. You reckon they should just get away with it?'

Jason didn't want to answer. Trying to get back at the loggers just seemed to make things more complicated. Mr Wherrett was right about that.

Einstein didn't wait for a response. ' 'Cause you undid our previous attack, we figured you'd wanna help with our next one.'

That didn't sound like an apology. In fact, Einstein seemed to be trying to make Jason feel apologetic because he took the punishment for vandalising the sign.

'What about the quolls?' asked Jason. 'Can't we just get rid of the loggers that way?'

Einstein grabbed a men's magazine and swatted a cockroach. 'That's Gillian's wussy approach. We gotta *hurt* 'em.' He banged his empty beer can down on the remains of the cockroach then lobbed it towards the overflowing bin. It bounced off the side and rolled away, joining several of its predecessors.

The gronk pulled a fresh can from the pack under his seat and offered one to Jason. Jason politely declined.

'Suit yourself. Look, you gotta play dirty in life. Life plays dirty with you. See how your mate Graham Lindsay looked after you.'

Jason would have preferred not to have been reminded about that. He clenched his jaw. 'What are you going to do?'

Einstein paused. 'We need your car.'

'You want to drive my Predator?' Jason thought for a few seconds. 'You want to get to the loggers' depot.'

'We won't hurt it. Your car, that is.'

'What about Tom's X-Trail?'

Einstein looked away. 'He won't be there. He'll be looking after his sick granny in the Tasmanian forest.'

Jason doubted that Einstein was capable of driving sensibly but didn't quite know how to say 'no'.

'That car isn't a toy,' said Einstein. 'It must be bored shitless going around the same old track all the time.'

'I know how it feels,' murmured Jason.

Einstein straightened in his seat. 'Well, you know what you could do, then. It'll be totally dark and no-one will be around. And it's not like we could dob you in.'

Jason looked out a window. It wasn't as though he'd be driving unsupervised, and Einstein was right about playing dirty. The PM definitely played dirty. This was a way for Jason to do it too—and in real dirt.

'What would I have to do?'

'Just drive. Me and the boys will do the rest.'

'Okay.'

●　　●　　●

Jason spent most of Thursday wondering what he'd let himself in for. He didn't get a job just so he could spend his petrol money being Einstein's chauffeur. At least being Einstein's chauffeur will be more exciting than being Bull's footstool. The opportunity to drive for real was a dream come true, but it was a shame that the circumstances weren't a bit less controversial.

After dinner, Jason found a spreadsheet program on the internet. This one was simpler than the school's one, so maybe it would be easier to get the hang of. It was also a bit slow, but at least it was free.

Raised voices in the hall interrupted Jason's concentration. It sounded like Mr Saunders was arguing with someone at the front door again. 'You're not welcome here' was clearly audible.

Jason was summoned to the lounge room. Mr Wherrett and Jason's parents were there, all standing and looking unhappy. The orange glow from the fireplace augmented the red in Mr Saunders' face.

'I came to thank you for the excellent job you did cleaning our sign,' said Mr Wherrett.

Jason nodded.

'And I remembered our discussion about the science behind what we're doing.'

Jason nodded again.

'I thought you might like some more information about it.'

Jason remained expressionless.

'May I sit down?' Mr Wherrett asked Jason's father. Mr Saunders didn't react, but Jason's mother motioned towards the lounge suite. The logger sat, and Jason lowered himself onto an adjacent recliner.

Mr Wherrett extracted some brochures and booklets from his briefcase and laid them out on the coffee table. He explained what each one was, and pointed out various pictures and graphs that supposedly showed how great thinning was.

'Oh yeah?' said Jason's father. 'And what will you be doing with the trees you cut down?'

'It would be silly to waste them, so they'll be used for paper production.'

'So you'll be making a profit by wrecking one of our tourist attractions. You're just taking money from us.'

'Mr Saunders, we're not wrecking anything. We're making it better.'

'What about the quolls Jason found?' asked Mrs Saunders.

Mr Wherrett nodded solemnly. 'If there really are quolls, we'll rethink things. We're taking that very seriously.' He took out more paperwork and placed it in front of Jason. It was a computer printout that listed all the reported sightings of quoll droppings.

Mr Saunders grunted and went to tend the fire. 'You couldn't spare us another log, could you?'

'Mr Saunders, like I said before, that wasn't us. No matter what the lady lawyer keeps saying on TV.'

'Are you sure it wasn't Roscoe?' asked Jason.

'Don't worry about him. I've got him on a leash.'

After Jason's father had ushered the visitor out the front door, Jason took the bundle of information he'd been given to his room, trying to be discreet about it so his father didn't think to add it to the fire. There was always a chance it contained some numbers that the thinning equations needed. It might even be possible to prove Mr Wherrett was lying about thinning by using his own information!

As Jason lay in bed that evening, he tried to work out what the point of the logger's visit was. He was bound to be up to something, but what? At least with Einstein, what he was up to was always obvious.

•　　•　　•

As Jason had suggested, Einstein turned up at Mr McKenzie's field on Saturday morning. He wasn't willing to let Jason drive on the next mission unless he was satisfied Jason was good enough, but there was no way Jason was going to let Einstein anywhere near his Predator's steering wheel.

During their first orbit of the paddock, Jason had to put up with a constant stream of driving advice from Einstein. That seemed a bit funny since the greenie had just trashed his own car. It was also funny that the greenies used to criticise Jason for driving, but things were different now they needed him.

Jason picked up the pace, to show his passenger he was totally competent. Driving in the forest was going to be great.

'Whoa,' said Einstein. 'You don't wanna lose it.'

'We'll have to get out of the forest quickly if the depot's got an alarm.'

'If you prang, we won't be going nowhere.'

Jason backed off a bit, even though he knew the Predator was good for more. 'So when are we going to do this?'

Einstein made a farting sound with his tongue. 'The others want to wait and see if the loggers give up. But if them arseholes are up to something, we're on.'

After a couple of sedate laps, Einstein had run out of useless suggestions. He'd also failed to notice that Jason had been edging his speed up again. Jason figured he should demonstrate what his Predator could *really* do, since that was the whole point of using it in the forest. Einstein was obviously used to a two-wheel-drive and had no idea.

They were finally getting up to a speed where it was fun. Jason crabbed the vehicle around a corner, almost daring the tyres to lose their grip, then glanced across to see if Einstein was impressed.

Unfortunately, Einstein seemed to have lost interest and was staring out the side window. 'Okay, last lap,' he said.

With only one decent turn to go, it made sense to push the car to the limit. Otherwise its full potential wouldn't be known and that could mean wasting time during the getaway.

As they entered the corner, Jason spun the steering wheel hard left—but the car didn't turn at all. The front tyres slid across the dirt like they were on ice. The wheels on the right side hit the embankment beside the track and the car tottered. Everything seemed to happen in slow motion like a replay of a wicket on TV. Jason had ample time to remember the previous times he'd tipped the

Predator up on two wheels; it had come back every other time so why wouldn't it come back now?

But the car kept on tipping. It fell onto its side while still speeding forward, delivering Jason a heavy bump on the temple. The roof line dug into the uneven ground and the roll continued until the vehicle finally came to rest the right way up.

Jason's head hurt. He fumbled with his seat belt but couldn't undo it. Everything seemed dim and distant. He looked across to see if his passenger was okay and was confused to see an empty seat. Had Einstein gone through the windscreen? No, his door was open. Forcing his eyes to focus through the haze, Jason identified Einstein's stocky figure running away. It vaulted the fence and was gone.

Chapter 15

Deep-fried Chips

The Predator was hurt much worse than its driver was. Jason had a few bumps and bruises, but the car's windscreen was broken and its roofline was pretty gruesome. To make sure Jason didn't try to start the engine, Mr Saunders had confiscated the keys. Worse, he said he didn't have the money to pay for repairs.

Neither did Jason, of course. After a lot of trial and error, he'd managed to get the spreadsheet program to tell him how long he'd have to work for to save up enough. Unless he'd made a mistake, it was almost two years.

The battered vehicle had been pushed into its carport. Its mutilated appearance hacked at Jason's insides whenever he walked up the driveway and saw it. It was as though the Predator was in pain and nobody was going to help it. After a few days, Jason found an old torn tarpaulin and threw it over the car just so he couldn't see it.

Then there was the problem of Mr Lindsay. Jason wondered whether he should tell the PM what had happened. After all, it was his car, sort of.

Jason's father didn't think it was necessary because the politician had given the car to Jason, so it wasn't any of his business any more. Anyway, Mr Lindsay seemed to have bigger problems to deal with at the moment. Reporters on TV were hassling him about his wimping out of the Rotterdam emission control agreement, since some other countries were also pulling out now and they were saying they were simply following Australia's example. Mr Lindsay tried to squirm out of it by saying Australia wasn't responsible for what they did.

News like that made Jason glad to be out of the climate change game. It just kept getting messier and messier.

Another game he was now out of was Einstein's mission to the loggers' depot. Since the Predator couldn't be used, Einstein would have to make other arrangements. The scumbag hadn't even tried to find out how badly Jason had been hurt in the accident.

Since he didn't need petrol money any more, Jason figured there wasn't a lot of point continuing with his job at McDonald's. David was there when he showed up for his final shift. Jason figured that having a Predator-inflicted bump on the head made up for the one he'd given David, or at least it gave them something else in common.

'No more hooning sessions for a while,' Jason promised.

'That's okay,' replied David through a mouthful of burger.

'You wanna come over sometime and do that spreadsheet assignment? I've been practicing on them.'

'No thanks.'

'*Grand Theft Auto*, then?'

David put down his burger. 'You're getting too, um, weird for me, Jason.'

Jason blinked.

'You hang around with those low-life greenies,' continued David. 'And Bull. And you're a quitter.'

'Of course I'm a quitter. There's no point trying if whatever you do doesn't make any difference.'

'You can believe that if you want to. I don't.' David turned away and resumed his meal.

Jason took the hint and left him alone.

●　　●　　●

David picked a bad time to get pissy. The winter holidays were an excellent time for computer games, and they weren't as much fun on your own.

At first, Jason tried racing against his father, but that was pretty much like racing on your own except you had to overtake him every time you lapped him.

Then there was on-line. There were thousands of players on-line, and most of them were pretty good. Jason made a few on-line racing friends and started advancing up the rankings.

Unfortunately, after a few days of intense competition, things took a bad turn. Jason's internet connection, which was laggy at the best of times, became basically unusable on Saturday. Everything seemed fine with his computer, so he headed into the hall to turn the modem off and on.

Just as he was about to throw the switch, his father intercepted him. 'Do you realise you've used up our whole month's internet in less than a week?'

That explained it.

Jason was forbidden from using the internet for gaming—not that it would have been possible until next month's data allowance came through anyway. Strong language emanated from Mr Saunders' study since he was trying to use the internet to do some work for his business.

Emma came over on Sunday, supposedly to see how Jason's skull was healing. The dragon had refused to let her visit but she got permission from Tom, who was actually at home this weekend. He seemed to be off visiting his mother at least a couple of times every month, even though it meant flying across Bass Strait.

Jason tested Emma out on *Grand Theft Auto* but she was even worse than his father. She took her eyes off the screen whenever a bird landed on the feeding table outside Jason's window, inevitably resulting in a major accident followed by a fit of giggling. While the racing was a fail, hearing Emma laugh was pretty nice.

• • •

On the second Tuesday of the holidays, Jason went to McDonald's for lunch, just in case David was there and in a more reasonable mood. After ordering his meal, Jason told the store manager that service standards had really slacked off in the last week. The manager didn't think that was very funny.

David wasn't there, but Bull was. Bull was as bored as Jason, which came as a surprise to Jason since there would have been heaps of things Bull could have been vandalising or graffitiing.

'Want to play a computer game?' asked Jason, fully expecting Bull to sneer at the suggestion.

'Got anything about killing people?'

'*Grand Theft Auto: Los Romeros?* You can try to run down the pedestrians.'

Bull crinkled his nose. 'I played that two years ago. Got the new one?'

'My computer probably couldn't run it. And it's still ninety dollars.'

'You don't need money to get computer games.'

'Well, yeah.' Jason extracted the lettuce and gherkin from his burger and replaced them with a layer of fries. 'It's just—'

'It's piss-easy. I'll show you how.'

'I know how. It's just—'

'Look, you had a car, and now you don't. So this is just making up for that.'

Jason tried to make sense of Bull's logic but failed. It seemed like something Einstein would say. It was no wonder the school bullies had joined forces with the radical greenies.

Bull was insistent, and Jason figured it was the only way he was going to get a decent race any time soon, so after they'd finished eating they went to Jason's place. Mrs Saunders offered to make them some salad sandwiches to make up for the junk food they'd just eaten, but Jason pointed out that they'd had lots of healthy vegetables: chips, and salad in the burgers. He failed to mention he'd thrown most of the salad in the bin.

'Chips are fried, so they're bad too,' said Jason's mother as the pair headed for Jason's room.

Jason installed the program that could get *Grand Theft Auto* for free, then started downloading the game. The internet was still stupidly slow, but at least it didn't matter how big the download was because they were already over the limit.

'You'll need the license key,' said Bull. 'I'll get Greasy to send it to you.' He poked away at his phone.

The download was obviously going to take forever. Instead of staring at a basically stationary progress bar, Bull insisted on inspecting the damaged Predator. He was highly impressed and congratulated Jason on his achievement.

Just as they came back inside, Jason got a text from Greasy with the license key. The download had finished, so he rushed through the installation process. If the game looked as good in reality as it did on YouTube, it was going to be awesome.

Jason allowed Bull to double-click the icon to start it running. An hourglass appeared for a few seconds, then an error message popped up:

```
Your computer does not meet the
minimum requirements to run this
program. Please refer to the
information printed on the product's
box.
```

'That's dumb,' said Bull, bashing the monitor hard enough to make it wobble. 'We don't *have* the box.'

Jason scanned through the programs on his computer. 'It'll be the CPU. There's something I can try....'

After digging through a few folders, he found the program he wanted. A window appeared, titled *Spectre Overclocking Utility*. It had copious buttons and sliders on it, but not much information about what anything meant.

Jason changed a few settings that seemed appropriate then clicked OK. A flashing red message appeared:

```
Warning !! Overclocking computer chip
may happen temporary or forever
damage !! Sure to continue ?
```

'Of course sure,' said Jason, clicking on the Yes button. After the computer restarted, he double-clicked the GTA icon—and got exactly the same error message as before.

'That's okay,' said Bull. 'It's nearly tea time anyway.'

'No. I'm going to get this to work. I didn't spend the afternoon downloading it for nothing.'

'You *did* download it for nothing, actually.'

'You know what I mean,' said Jason, peering again at the overclocking utility's settings. He made a couple of adjustments and tried to save the changes, but another warning popped up:

```
The setting's you selected may not
stable unless chip voltage increase .
Want to do ?
```

'Yeees,' Jason told the computer sarcastically. The warning about damage appeared again but Jason clicked it away, waited impatiently while the machine woke up again, then restarted GTA.

The hourglass lingered for longer this time. Jason glared at the screen, daring it to tell him the computer still wasn't fast enough.

GTA's opening cut-scene started.

'Yes!' said Jason. He skipped over the cut-scene and a beaten-up pink station wagon appeared. He jumped in and floored it. The car lurched onto the wrong side of the road then mounted the curb, forcing a dozen pedestrians to leap for their virtual lives.

'Missed 'em,' said Bull.

'It's the frame rate. It stutters.'

'Is that how come you totalled your Predator too?'

'I didn't total it.' Jason got back onto the road and roared past a bunch of cars waiting at a red traffic light. The station wagon's reflection was visible in the duco of the other cars as it overtook them.

Bull prodded Jason on the shoulder. 'When do I get a go?'

'When I've finished testing it.' A huge American police car lurched out of a side street and accelerated after Jason.

'What's that sound?' asked Bull.

'Cop car.' Jason ducked down an alley to try to evade it.

Bull reached in front of Jason and pressed the Esc key. The game paused, leaving dented garbage cans hanging in mid-air.

Jason stopped pounding the keyboard and glared at Bull. 'I'll give you a go soon, okay?'

'Listen.'

Even though the game was frozen, a siren was still audible. 'That's odd,' said Jason. 'It shouldn't do that.'

The alarm only lasted a couple of seconds before the screen went blank and the speakers fell silent, leaving only the sound of the computer's fan.

'That don't sound good,' said Bull.

Jason tried to restart the computer, but nothing happened. The power-on test blurb didn't even appear. He went through the ritual three times before giving up. 'Dad's going to kill me,' he said.

'What's up with it?'

'The CPU chip must have got cooked from the overclocking.' Jason punched himself on the side of the head.

'Looks like your mum was right.'

'My mum? She doesn't have a clue about computers.'

'She warned you about fried chips.'

Chapter 16

Computer Games

Jason tossed the info about thinning that Mr Wherrett had given him onto his bed, then flopped down beside it and started skimming. Most of it was glossy and colourful, but it wasn't specifically about Sapphire Forest and it didn't provide the numbers that the thinning equations needed. It was basically just advertising. No wonder the loggers needed to cut down trees for paper if they wasted it on stuff like this.

On closer inspection, Jason found he could read some numbers off the graphs. They were a lot different to the guesses he'd made when he'd tried to crunch the equations before; maybe different enough to get rid of the circular reference issue, whatever that was. But without a computer, there was no way to find out.

If he was going to get a new computer, it had to be a good one. Any old computer could run a spreadsheet, but games were another matter. It would need a fast CPU and a powerful graphics card. Based on recent experience, some heavy-duty cooling fans would be a good idea too. All up, it would probably cost about $2,000. The money from Mr Wherrett—if he ever coughed up—was only half way there.

Jason got out his calculator and tried to figure out how long he'd have to work to save up that much. Going back to a calculator after using a spreadsheet was a pain because you had to start again whenever you made a mistake or wanted to try something different. The final answer came out at about four months. Half the forest could be gone by then.

A picture of a quoll caught Jason's eye. One of Mr Wherrett's docs was a whole report just about quolls. It had more numbers about quolls than all the other docs had about trees. A table even listed the dates and locations of all the poo sightings. Jason's find was in there, as well as the one Emma dumped in his hand and the two Tom had lost. Mr Wherrett was certainly serious about the quolls.

• • •

It seemed wrong to be glad when school started again, but school had Emma—and working computers. After English with Ms Gow, Jason skipped IT and went to the library. He couldn't resist trying the thinning equations with the numbers he'd scraped from Mr Wherrett's handouts.

The computer rejected Jason's first attempt to log on, so he typed his password more carefully. That got rejected too. He tried another computer, but still no go.

As Jason was checking the network cables, David strode in. He sat down in front of a computer without saying anything.

'Network's down,' said Jason.

'We'll see.'

Jason walked over to watch David's attempt to log in fail.

It didn't.

'How come it didn't work for me?' demanded Jason, as though it was David's fault somehow.

'Did you renew your IT account, like Chandra said in class?'

'How could I possibly have known about that?'

David shrugged his shoulders and got on with his work.

This was a setback. Without an IT account, there was no way to get access to all the good stuff on the network. You could browse the internet and the library catalogue, but that was about it. No spreadsheet, no multimedia apps, and no way to do IT assignments.

Visiting Dr Chandrasekhar probably wouldn't work. Jason doubted that the teacher would renew his account unless he started turning up to class a bit more often.

Fortunately, there was another way to get into the IT area. Jason waited until David left and then logged in using his ex-friend's user name and password, which he'd found out by watching David type them in. It served David right for not being more security-conscious.

• • •

'Dad, don't!' begged Jason. 'Please!'

'I hope I don't have to,' said Mr Saunders, smearing a generous layer of Vegemite on his morning toast. 'But unless things pick up, I won't be able to pay her.'

Jason continued to plead even though he knew it was pointless. Mr Saunders' factory was losing money, and this wouldn't be the first time he'd had to sack someone this year.

But why did it have to be Bull's mum?

Obviously Jason's parents weren't going to be contributing to his new computer fund. Not that they even knew the full extent of the problem with the machine; Jason had avoided going into details in case the whole story came out. They wouldn't be impressed if they found out about the pirated software. He could always try the 'everybody else does it' defence but that didn't sound so convincing any more, since that was the PM's excuse for allowing greenhouse gas pollution and even he was having trouble getting away with it.

●　　●　　●

Being able to use David's log-in details at school meant Jason had some computer access, even if it wasn't as convenient as having a computer at home. He spent an hour or two in his corner of the library most days, dividing his time between spreadsheeting, assignments and browsing the web.

It took him a few days to reconstruct his tree thinning spreadsheet on the school's system. Annoyingly, the values he'd extracted from Mr Wherrett's info didn't cure the circular reference error. A Google search for 'circular reference' got millions of hits but none that made any sense.

To give his brain a break from circular references one afternoon, Jason browsed to a computer game forum. Over the top of his monitor, he saw David come into the library. Surprisingly, David strode straight over to Jason's corner, although the fierce expression on his face suggested it wasn't going to be a purely social call.

'Chandra's just suspended me from IT,' David said loudly.

'I told you there was no point sitting through classes,' replied Jason, relieved that David was finally talking to him again.

'He suspended me for misusing the school's computers. Looking at web sites I've never even heard of. You wouldn't know anything about that, would you?'

Jason's chest felt tight. 'I didn't know this would happen.'

'You going to fess up?'

Jason looked down but didn't answer straight away. He couldn't see any neat way out of this. Someone was going to get suspended and he didn't want it to be him. He wanted to pass IT—just not sit through boring classes. But David hadn't done anything wrong, so Jason nodded slowly.

'Stay there,' ordered David. 'And don't touch that computer.' He swept out of the library and returned within a minute, closely followed by Dr Chandrasekhar. The teacher dropped his bulbous body onto the seat beside Jason and looked expectantly at him.

'It was me,' said Jason.

Chandra remained expressionless. 'If you misuse school computers again, I will start the formal disciplinary process,' he said in his heavily-accented staccato.

'I guess it doesn't matter,' murmured Jason, waving an arm at the spreadsheet on his screen. 'I can't work it out anyway.'

'If you come to my class, you might learn.' The teacher leaned towards the monitor. 'What are you trying to do here?'

Jason tried not to react to the odour of tobacco that Chandra exuded, and explained about the tree thinning equations and Mr Wherrett's so-called data.

'Tell you what,' said Chandra, 'you come to my classes and I tell you about this.'

'You'll be covering this in class?' asked Jason.

'No. Not in class for a few years. You come to my staff room and I teach you.'

Jason figured he didn't have much choice. Turning down the offer would almost certainly mean suspension from IT and maths, which wouldn't go down well with his parents. So it was back to the grind.

•　　　•　　　•

Just before school next morning, Emma bounded up and blurted out the latest news. 'You did it! The loggers have admitted the poo you found is from an eastern quoll!'

'Woo hoo! So they can't log any more?'

Emma shrugged. 'How could they?'

Jason shrugged back. It seemed like game over for the loggers, with victory going to QAP. And the quolls, of course.

It was probably victory for Jason too. The loggers would have to pay out the $1,000 reward money. At least he could get a computer that would do for schoolwork and spreadsheets. Serious gaming would be out of the question.

If only they'd announced this a few days earlier! Jason would have just waited until he got a new computer instead of breaking into David's account, and then he wouldn't have had to spend extra time with Dr Chandrasekhar. And now the loggers had lost, he didn't need to get the thinning spreadsheet working because the thinning wasn't going to happen.

Still, it would be a relief to be able to prove that thinning was rubbish. Otherwise, QAP would have stopped the loggers from fixing up the forest. If the forest really was sick, leaving it alone could actually make it worse for the quolls in the future, and Jason didn't want to feel responsible for that.

After putting it off for a few days, Jason made an appointment to see Chandra about his extra spreadsheet lessons. He expected the doctor to point out a missing minus sign or something equally trivial, but instead he started talking about a kind of maths Jason had never heard of. The little man seemed like a whole different person: the droning voice was replaced by bubbling enthusiasm and there was copious arm-waving. The whiteboard in his corner of the staff room was soon covered in diagrams with symbols that weren't English, although they didn't look Indian either.[5]

At the end of the period, Chandra ferreted through the piles of books on the floor and eventually pulled one out and handed it over. *Great,* thought Jason, *more homework.*

• • •

Jason met Chandra during lunch time twice a week. The maths in the book was a major brain-strain; Jason had to ask lots of questions and even struggled with some of the revision problems. He was impatient for Chandra to start talking about the thinning equations, but the teacher never did. Jason guessed he'd forgotten how all this started.

One evening, after Jason got stuck on one of the problems in the textbook, he got out the thinning equations. They seemed different now. They looked like they could have come straight out of the textbook.

Finally it all made sense. Now Jason understood why the thinning equations linked back to themselves, and why the spreadsheet complained about circular references. He even had a theory about how to redesign the spreadsheet so it would work, but without a computer he couldn't try it out. That would have to wait until a spare lunch time at school, and now he was spending so many lunch times with Chandra, that didn't leave too many. He *really* needed a computer at home.

Mr Wherrett still hadn't come up with the grand he owed. He kept blaming 'head office' for not releasing the funds. The logger had also said something about doing a deal with Jason, but Jason didn't want a deal; he wanted a computer.

During his next session with Dr Chandrasekhar, Jason hoped he'd be allowed to spend the time rehashing his spreadsheet but the teacher wanted to keep talking about the maths. Once more he filled his whiteboard with boxes and arrows and other hieroglyphics. Jason turned his nose up at the pictures and pointed out that Mr Wherrett had tried to convince him about thinning by using images and graphs—but no numbers.

'Your logging friend is wise,' said the doctor. 'A graph can show things the numbers hide.'

Jason wasn't convinced.[6]

•　　　•　　　•

Next Wednesday evening, just as Jason was finishing up an essay for English, he was summoned to the lounge room. Mr Wherrett was there again, and this time he'd brought Roscoe.

Finally, my money, thought Jason. Roscoe was carrying a briefcase-sized satchel; surely they weren't going to pay him in cash, like in a ransom movie, were they?

'We heard you had a setback with your research,' said Mr Wherrett.

Jason didn't want to reply since he still didn't trust the logger, and the chainsaw wielder was even more of a worry. But since there was $1,000 at stake, Jason figured he'd better be nice, at least until they'd handed over the money. 'You mean my computer? How did you know?'

'I'm sorry about how long it's taking to get your money,' said Mr Wherrett, 'but maybe we can fix you up with something better, right now.' He motioned to Roscoe, who placed the satchel on the coffee table.

Following a nod from Mr Wherrett, Jason opened it. He reached inside and pulled out a surprisingly heavy laptop computer. It was as large as the monitor from his desktop computer.

'We had to order a bunch of these for the company,' explained Mr Wherrett. 'I tacked an extra one onto the order in case you were interested. But you can still hold out for a cheque if you'd rather.'

The laptop was a good brand, but it was bound to be a trick. It probably didn't work. 'Can I turn it on?' asked Jason.

Permission was granted, so Jason rummaged through the bag to see if the transformer was in there. It was, as well as something that looked like a USB memory stick on steroids.

'That's a mobile broadband modem,' said Mr Wherrett. 'We'll pay for your internet access. Just leave it plugged in all the time and you'll never have to worry about using up your Dad's internet.'

'We'll take it,' said Mr Saunders, giving Jason a dirty look.

The laptop woke up with a newer version of Windows than Jason was used to, so it took him a while to find out what sort of graphics chip it had. It actually had a full-on graphics card that was better than the one in his dead computer, as well as having more memory and a bigger disk drive.

'This would have cost more than $1,000,' said Jason.

Mr Wherrett nodded. 'A lot more. We specced it out with every option. You'd definitely be getting a good deal.'

Jason's father narrowed his eyes. 'What's in this for you?' he asked the logger.

'I'm happy to come clean,' said Mr Wherrett, standing with his palms forward. 'We know Jason's been researching what we're doing, and losing his computer must have been a setback. If he can continue, he'll find out for himself that what we're doing is good for the forest, and it would help our cause if the greenies' prize recruit came over to our side.'

'You're not still planning to log the forest, are you?' asked Mrs Saunders. 'You've admitted there's quolls in it.'

'That's up to the government. A smaller operation might still be possible.'

'A few overgrown rodents won't stop us,' added Roscoe. 'Get a clue.'

Mr Wherrett bashed his forehead with his hand. 'Quolls aren't rodents, blockhead. You knew that, didn't you, Jason?'

Jason did but he didn't want to admit it since Roscoe wasn't looking too happy, so he changed the subject. 'If I'm going to use the computer for what you said, I'll need a spreadsheet.'

Mr Wherrett knelt in front of the computer and brought up a spreadsheet program. He typed the name of a file to open but only got an error message:

```
File not found: qual.xls
```

'Did you mean Q U O L L?' asked Jason.

'Probably.' The logger typed 'quoll' and a table of quoll poo findings appeared. 'There we go. It's got all the data I printed out for you. Probably more.'

'What if I prove thinning is bad?'

'That'll only happen if you don't get your sums right,' said Mr Wherrett, winking. 'But you'd still get to keep the computer, no strings attached. Do we have a deal?'

Jason looked over to his parents, but they indicated it was up to him.

The machine had to be worth at least two grand, and that wasn't counting the free internet access. He could even take it to school and play games on it during the few lunch times Chandra let him have to himself. Everyone would be disgustingly jealous.

'Where do I sign?' asked Jason.

The logger placed a form in front of Jason and pointed. 'This is just to say you've taken the computer instead of the reward money,' he explained. Jason signed.

'I'll just enable your internet access,' said Mr Wherrett. He logged into the laptop using his own account while Jason watched. After getting some help with the spelling of Jason's surname, he created a network account for Jason, then he and Roscoe departed.

Jason's head was spinning. At tea time, the most powerful computer he owned was his phone. Now he probably had the best laptop in Sapphire Bay, and his new toy could probably drag off most desktops too.

Of course, even though it was free, there was still a price. Mr Wherrett obviously expected him to make a decision about whether logging was good or not, and that meant sorting out the spreadsheet once and for all. Not taking sides was proving almost impossible.

Mr Wherrett's utter confidence that Jason would come down in favour of thinning was also a worry. If the logger was right, he could kiss goodbye to Emma, at least figuratively.

Chapter 17

Graphic Evidence

Lousy Gow the Sow.

As if Jason didn't have enough homework to do already. Although he'd managed to recover most of his old computer's files from his internet backup, he still lost the most recent versions of some of his assignments as well as some stuff that hadn't been stored under `My Documents`.

And now Ms Gow wanted him to resubmit an essay just because he hadn't rammed an opinion down the reader's throat (or in their eye sockets). The teacher seemed to think there had to be a single answer to every question, but Jason always saw more.

After revising the first three pages of his essay, Jason decided to reward himself with a gaming session on his new laptop. The latest GTA would be a good test of its performance, and that meant downloading it again. But before the download completed, Mrs Saunders walked in so he quickly popped up his spreadsheet.

After assuring his mother he'd been working on his essay, Jason showed her the tree thinning spreadsheet, complete with circular reference error. Even though Mrs Saunders worked at a university she couldn't make any sense of it, but that was understandable since the spreadsheet didn't have many headings and its layout was as messy as Jason's schoolwork.

While his mother watched, Jason started to modify the spreadsheet based on his theory about how to cure the circular reference problem. He got so engrossed he didn't notice her leave.

It took over an hour, but it worked! No more circular references. The spreadsheet now happily predicted what would happen to the forest for as many years into the future as you wanted to go. Jason made it look five years ahead, then ten, then fifty. The spreadsheet did all the calculations so quickly you couldn't see it.[7]

Unfortunately, Jason's elation didn't last long. The spreadsheet said the number of trees would double within three years. That didn't seem right.

Jason guessed the problem was because some of the numbers didn't apply to Sapphire Forest. The docs Mr Wherrett had given him were about thinning in general, and the graphs in them were labelled 'typical example' and things like that. Maybe Sapphire Forest wasn't typical. Jason tried changing a few values by just a bit, and it made a huge difference. The spreadsheet was obviously a fussy eater.

Gillian might have better numbers. Back when all this started, she had a report that was all about thinning in Sapphire Forest. But if Jason asked her about it, she might mention it to Tom, and Tom would probably tell Emma. That would result in questions Jason didn't want to have to answer.

Of course, the loggers were bound to have a copy of that report. Mr Wherrett had said there was more info about thinning on the laptop. Unfortunately, looking for it would have to wait until Ms Gow had been appeased.

● ● ●

Dr Chandrasekhar was impressed with Jason's new spreadsheet. He spent ages poring over it but couldn't find any mistakes, although he did say the spreadsheet would be easier to understand if it were laid out better. He agreed that its strange predictions were probably caused by bad data.

Jason didn't get around to looking for better data for a few days. When he finally got time, he headed straight for Jason's Documents on his laptop. It had a folder called Thinning, but that only contained electronic versions of the docs Mr Wherrett had already handed over. So where was the extra stuff?

A wider search was obviously required. A folder called \\AFI looked interesting. The computers at school had some folders starting with \\, and they provided access to the files on the school's network.

\\AFI had three folders in it. The first one was named FW, and it contained files called Education&Coarses.doc and WorkExperiance.doc. This must be Mr Wherrett's personal info. The man had a serious problem with spelling. Jason initially wondered why Mr Wherrett's files were on his computer, but then he realised he was probably accessing some other computer on the network.

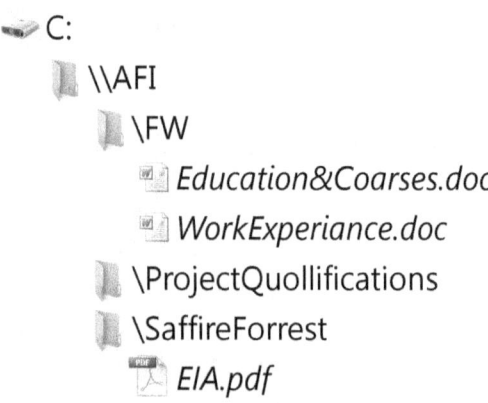

C:
  \\AFI
    \FW
      Education&Coarses.doc
      WorkExperiance.doc
    \ProjectQuollifications
    \SaffireForrest
      EIA.pdf

The name of the second folder under \\AFI made Jason laugh. It was ProjectQuollifications. This was obviously another one or Mr Wherrett's personal folders, so Jason didn't look in it.

The third folder, SaffireForrest, was the jackpot. It contained over a hundred files. The largest one was called EIA.pdf, and it took almost a minute to open, probably because of the network. Mostly it was just words, but buried in the back were some appendixes that contained heaps of measurements from Sapphire Forest. There was way too much information to wade through in a single evening, so Jason saved a copy of the document onto his laptop's hard drive. That way, he could open it more quickly in future. He named it Numbers.pdf since EIA.pdf wasn't a very descriptive filename.

• • •

Jason started going through Numbers.pdf on Sunday. It took hours to sift through the appendixes and pick out the numbers that seemed relevant. When the chore was complete, he opened up the spreadsheet to put the new numbers into it. The spreadsheet seemed a bit different to how he remembered it: it was clearer somehow. There were more headings and better formatting. Jason was impressed that a computer program could work out how to do things like that all by itself.

More importantly, the new numbers seemed to work. The computer predicted the forest would slowly decline over the next few decades. Nothing sudden or drastic happened. At last, a believable result.

As a test, Jason adjusted the spreadsheet so that it had fewer big trees at the start, like what the loggers were proposing to do. This time, the forest went along fine, which is exactly what the ecological thinning web sites said should happen. The equations had put up a good fight, but Jason had finally beaten them.

The satisfaction of mastering the maths suddenly gave way to the horrible realisation that Mr Wherrett had been right all along.

Jason realised he shouldn't be surprised that a professional in a forestry company knew more about managing forests than a bunch of protesters did. The greenies were good at making a lot of noise but they didn't really know much. It was lucky for them that they chose to focus on quolls rather than trees.

It seemed like a contest: the health of the quolls versus the health of the forest. Jason wondered whether he could be on the greenies' side about the quolls but on the loggers' side about the trees.

Was it too late to go back to being on nobody's side about anything? This was beyond messy; just another situation in which it was better not to have an opinion. And if you can't help but have an opinion, at least keep it to yourself.

Unfortunately, there were two small problems with that. Emma was one. Fighting beside Emma for the quolls had been a buzz.

The other problem was Mr Wherrett. Jason's thinning research was sort of a condition of him getting the laptop. The logger would want to know what Jason had concluded.

Maybe he wouldn't make a big deal out of it.

●   ●   ●

About twenty reporters were present. That was way more than there was in Sapphire Bay; Mr Wherrett must have invited some from further away. Jason tried to keep his head up but it just wanted to point at the dirt. It's as though it had a mind of its own. Which it did, of course.

Mr Wherrett had asked Jason to look confident, but there was nothing Jason could do about the redness of his face. He'd assured the logger it would be better for both of them if he wasn't in front of the cameras at all, but Mr Wherrett wouldn't buy that. The deal they ended up striking was that Mr Wherrett would do all the talking, and Jason would just … stand there.

It didn't help that the press conference was in the picnic area where the quoll search had left from. Jason felt like a traitor. The trees behind him responded to the wind with a ghostly whoosh, as if they knew that Jason had condemned some of them. He fought to remind himself that this was for the forest's own good. Maybe not now, but in the future.

Mr Wherrett was having a field day. Literally. He waved his arms at the bushland and pulled up handfuls of weeds for the cameras. Jason was standing as far behind him as he thought he could get away with, and the strong breeze made it hard to make out what the logger was saying. Every now and then, Mr Wherrett would turn around and wave an arm at Jason, looking as proud as if he'd just given birth.

While Mr Wherrett was speaking, one of the other loggers handed out printouts from Jason's spreadsheet to the reporters. Jason wondered where the printouts had come from since he'd never made any. Maybe one of his parents, who were shivering in the background, had done it. The handouts looked pretty professional since they were on glossy A3-sized card, and the spreadsheet's auto-formatting had added colours to some of the results: green for good and red for bad.

Mr Wherrett obviously had no idea about Einstein's plan to attack his depot. By bragging to the media, the logger was playing with fire but he didn't realise it. Jason hoped this development wouldn't be the trigger that propelled Einstein and his mates into action. If it was, that would make Jason responsible in a way, since it was his spreadsheet Mr Wherrett was crapping on about. But he didn't really have any choice: the spreadsheet said what it said, and numbers can't lie.

The event concluded with a burst of camera flashes as Mr Wherrett shook Jason's hand for the fourth time that morning. A couple of reporters made moves towards Jason but Mr Wherrett turned them back.

After waving off the last of his guests, Mr Wherrett thanked Jason for putting up with the event. 'You're still not comfortable with what we're doing, are you?' he asked.

'There's still the quolls.'

'So there is. I'm going to update our plans to make sure we don't interfere with them. But if we don't keep the forest healthy, they really will go extinct from here in the future.' Mr Wherrett flicked a finger against the left-over printouts he was holding. 'You proved that yourself.'

Jason nodded but his gaze fell to the ground again.

'You shouldn't be ashamed of your work,' said the logger. 'I never expected anything as good as this!'

'I just used the info you gave me on the computer. It was really good. Especially the, um, EI something.'

'*That* was on your computer?'

'Yep. Well, on the network.'

'Oh, of course. You did well to find it.'

After being conditioned to dislike Mr Wherrett for so long, Jason found it difficult to accept that the logger was actually a reasonable guy. After all, he didn't *have* to shield Jason from the reporters. It would have been better for him if Jason had spoken to them. There was still the strange matter of the log through the window, but maybe Mr Wherrett wasn't in on that. Roscoe could have done it off his own bat.

Before the press conference, Jason had told Gillian that he couldn't be in QAP any more. She was obviously very disappointed. Tom's reaction was also predictable: he banned Jason from visiting Emma. Not that that really made any difference since there's no way Emma would have anything more to do with a defector like Jason. Jason realised he'd have to avoid her at school from now on, in case she felt like dumping crap in his hands again—but this time, it probably *would* be from a dog.

Even Jason's father was unimpressed with Jason's about-face. He didn't try to find mistakes in the spreadsheet, but pointed out that it didn't take into account the impact on tourism and other local businesses. By which he meant his own business, of course. Jason could imagine Tom saying exactly the same thing.

●　　●　　●

Dr Chandrasekhar held his face close to the screen and scrolled up and down the spreadsheet. 'You are right, I think. I like the new layout, too.'

'Actually, the auto-format did that,' Jason explained.

'The what?'

'You know, where the spreadsheet changes itself automatically.'

Chandra looked sceptical. 'I did not know it could do that.'

'Trust me,' said Jason. 'I don't make things look neat on my own.'

'That much I believe. So it is very pretty, but can you explain why the forest behaves like this?'

Jason cocked his head to one side and stared at the screen of numbers. 'I don't get the question. It just does.'

'Do the trees solve equations? Or is that only for smart students with good teachers?'

Jason kept looking at the data but it didn't help.

'No,' continued Chandra, 'the forest does what it does for *reasons*. For *causes*. To understand, we need to know more than *what* will happen. We need to know *why*.'

'Okay, so … what?'

'The answer is probably in there,' said Chandra, waving a hand at the monitor, 'but we cannot see the forest for the trees.' He chuckled at his own joke.

Jason didn't think the joke justified a response.

'*Graphs*, Mr Saunders! *Show* me what is happening. A picture is worth a thousand numbers.'

'Pictures are useless,' said Jason. 'That's all the loggers gave me at first. They don't prove anything.'

Dr Chandrasekhar swivelled Jason's laptop towards himself and started hammering on the keyboard. His stubby fingers moved so fast that Jason couldn't follow them. Detecting the teacher's password would have been impossible.

A graph appeared. It had a solid line for the total number of trees and a dotted line for the rate at which new seedlings sprang up. Interestingly, the lines looked a bit similar. Jason bent forward to take a closer look, but Chandra deleted the graph before Jason could work out what it was telling him.

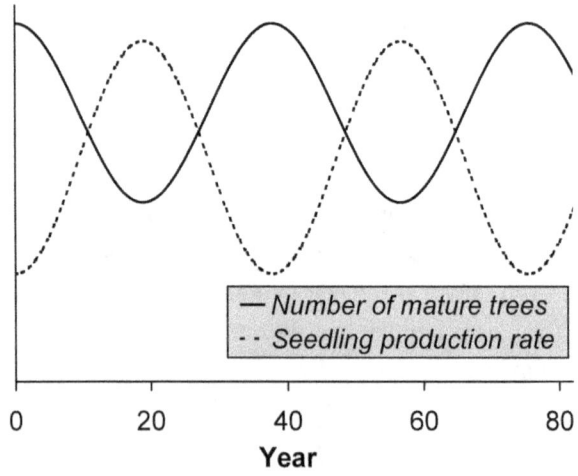

'Believe me now?' asked the teacher.

'Maybe, but I hadn't finished looking at it. Can you put it back?'

'No. You need to learn how to do them.'

'Easy.' Jason clicked on the Graph button, but things got out of control after that. While Chandra leaned back and smiled, Jason stabbed hopefully at a few options, then clicked Finish. The resulting graph was nothing like Chandra's. Jason's creation didn't make any sense at all.

'Always you run before you walk,' said the teacher. 'Graph something simple. That is your homework.'

• • •

It was convenient that Chandra had referred to his request as 'homework'. Jason knew it wasn't really homework because it wasn't part of any course, but if he thought of it as homework then he could justify playing with his spreadsheet instead of doing his next English essay.

Again and again he tried to create a graph like the one Chandra had made, but each time it came out wrong. Just as he was getting close to throwing his laptop across the room, he got a text from Mr Wherrett:

Been looking at qual data but cant see any patern to it. Maybe u can!

Jason figured he'd done enough for the logger's cause and went back to his spreadsheet, but then remembered what Chandra had said about graphing something simple. Maybe he could kill two birds with one stone. He opened the quoll data file and studied it. Like Mr Wherrett said, there wasn't any obvious pattern. Before this year, the last confirmed sighting in Sapphire Forest was two decades ago. There'd been occasional unconfirmed sightings since then but they seemed pretty suss. Not surprisingly, the most detailed info was for the finds that he and Tom had made.

Jason's first thought was to try to graph the locations of the quoll poo findings, but then realised it would be even easier to graph their dates. He pasted the data from Mr Wherrett's table into a new spreadsheet and went through the graphing process once more.

As usual, the graph he produced looked like rubbish. It was four spikes more-or-less evenly spaced over the time line. Jason bashed the side the screen as hard as he dared, then went back to look at the numbers to work out what he'd stuffed up.

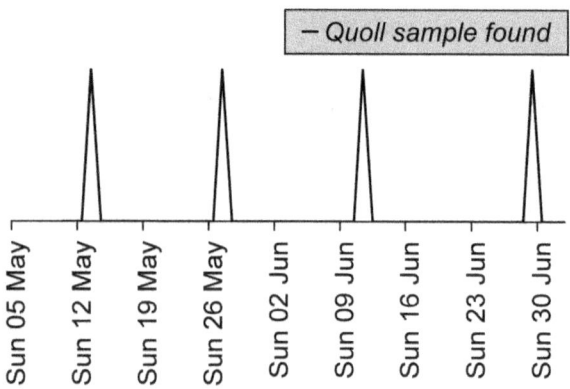

He hadn't stuffed anything up. The graph wasn't lying. The spikes were exactly on the dates of the quoll poo sightings. There was one about every two weeks.

Every two weeks. Jason added a new column to the spreadsheet, then started looking through the old messages on his phone. Emma's texts were especially helpful, but even one from Bull was relevant since it pinned down the date they'd graffitied the sign.

When he'd found all the dates he was looking for, Jason added them to the graph on his spreadsheet. Four new spikes appeared, drawn with dotted lines. They were close to the original spikes, but they occurred a few days earlier and fell on every second weekend. That was what Jason expected, although it definitely wasn't what he wanted.

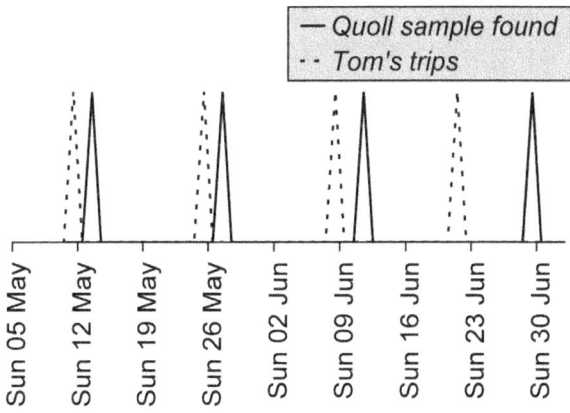

One thing still didn't make sense. How could anyone collect poo from an extinct animal? Jason pulled up Wikipedia's page on quolls and skimmed it. The explanation leapt out at him: eastern quolls were only thought to be extinct *on the mainland*. There were lots in Tasmania.

But Jason himself had found one of the samples, and he'd found it in Sapphire Forest! He cast his mind back to the quoll search event and bit his lower lip. Rather than disproving his terrible theory, the events of that day actually supported it.

Tom was getting quoll poo from Tasmania and making out that it came from Sapphire Forest.

Chapter 18

Where There's Smoke...

Failed again.

Jason sat on the end of his bed and read what Ms Gow had scrawled on his last essay:

Once again, you haven't drawn any conclusions. You didn't try to convince me about anything. As a favour, I'll give you one last chance. You may submit one more essay, on a topic of your choice.

'A favour'? Since when was having to write more essays than anyone else in the class 'a favour'? If this was a favour, the sow's punishments must be foul.

Jason tried to think of a topic for his penalty essay, even though the answer was obvious. He'd spent the last few days convincing himself that he should forget about Tom and the quoll poo dates. It was probably just a coincidence. Blabbing about it would just risk being proved wrong, and it wasn't like the thinning spreadsheet situation where he was obliged to tell someone.

Then there was Emma. She'd been surprisingly cool about the thinning spreadsheet. She'd demanded to know what it was, and Jason had carefully explained. Although she wasn't convinced, she was willing to accept that Jason believed what he believed for good reasons, rather than just being pure evil.

It was one thing to suggest that a few trees should be cut down, but accusing someone's father of cheating was heavier. Jason reminded himself that this was only a school assignment, so there was no way Emma could find out what he wrote. It would just be between him and the sow.

Writing about Tom would also be a kind of insurance. If the greenies went through with their plan to attack the depot, Jason could honestly say he'd told an adult the greenies were corrupt, so nobody could accuse him of being on their side. The punishment essay was an opportunity to get his secret off his chest without exactly dobbing on anyone.

He created a new word processor document, then stared at the blank screen. This would have been so much easier if he still thought everything was simple and one-sided, like when he was fighting the PM about global warming. For the sake of his English assessment, he tried to recapture that feeling and started pounding on the keyboard.

●　　　●　　　●

Ms Gow only took one day to mark the essay. She dropped it on Jason's desk at the end of class.

Your worst effort yet. This is supposed to be English, not maths. If this is your idea of convincing people, you're better off keeping your thoughts to yourself.

That's what I've been trying to tell you all along, thought Jason. He was staring so hard at Ms Gow's oh-so-neat comment that he didn't notice Bull reading it over his shoulder.

'Epic fail,' said Bull. 'Welcome to the club.'

Jason jumped. He'd been trying to avoid Bull. But the thug seemed calm enough, so Mr Saunders can't have told Bull's mother the bad news yet.

After Bull trudged off, it was Emma's turn. 'Failed again?' she asked.

Jason nodded. 'Lousy Sow. She hates me.'

'She isn't *that* bad. What was it about?' Emma craned her skinny neck to try to see the essay but Jason shoved it into his bag.

'Nothing.'

'Then it's not surprising you failed. No really, what?'

Jason decided to test Emma. 'What if the quoll poo wasn't for real? Like, it was all a sham.'

'Sham poo? I'm never going to wash my hair again.'

'You mean you do now?'

Emma delivered a surprisingly powerful blow to Jason's shoulder. 'Of course the poo is real. My dad found most of it.'

Emma clearly had total faith in Tom. Since she knew her father better than Jason did, that should count for something. Emma's trust in her dad had to be balanced against Jason's dwindling trust in his spreadsheet. Maybe Ms Gow had been right to fail the essay.

●　　●　　●

Dr Chandrasekhar's corner of the staff room ponged more than usual. 'So how did you go with your homework?' asked the teacher.

Before he'd got sidetracked, Jason had only managed to create a single spreadsheet graph—the one that showed the dates of the quoll poo findings alongside the dates of Tom's trips to Tasmania. Reluctantly, he opened it up.

Chandra spent at least a minute frowning at the graph, with his nose less than a ruler-length away from the screen. 'Do you know what this means?' he asked eventually.

'It doesn't mean anything,' said Jason. He pulled his crumpled English essay out of his bag and handed it to the maths teacher.

Chandra read Ms Gow's red ink, then flipped through the essay and read the conclusion. 'Maybe this is not a good essay. I would not know. But you must not let this "Mr J" get away with it. Have you showed your parents?'

Jason shook his head. His dad wouldn't agree with anything that supported the loggers, and his mother wouldn't react well to yet another failed assignment.

'If you do not come forward with this, I will have to,' said the teacher, frowning again. 'But you should do it. You should get credit.'

I should get the blame for being wrong, you mean, thought Jason.

Unfortunately, the only way to stop Dr Chandrasekhar from blabbing about the quoll poo seemed to be for Jason to do it himself, so he promised he would. At least that would buy some time to work out what—if anything—was really going on.

•　　•　　•

Jason managed to put off showing anyone else his graph for a week. The government still hadn't made an announcement about whether they were going to allow thinning to proceed, and Einstein still hadn't made a move against the loggers' depot. Jason was tempted to do nothing in the hope it would all just go away.

It didn't. On Friday, Emma reported that the greenies were raving about some accusation the loggers had made, but she didn't know any details because Tom was away again. Jason feared the worst: Chandra must have told the loggers what Tom had been doing.

'Einstein said it's about what they wrote on that log,' said Emma.

' "Butt out u little arsehole else next 1 will be on fire",' recited Jason. One doesn't quickly forget what's written on logs thrown through one's bedroom window.

Neither of them could work out how that message was relevant, although it was always difficult to follow Einstein's logic. Jason's best guess was that Einstein was still on about getting revenge against the loggers for throwing the log, although that didn't have anything to do with the message on the log, nor with the loggers accusing Tom.

As he was trying to get to sleep that night, Jason suddenly thought of another possible explanation for Einstein's comment. Maybe the greenie was planning to do what the log had threatened, and heave a burning successor to it through Jason's window! That made perfect sense: Einstein despised Jason for crossing over to the loggers, and if he knew that Jason was responsible for exposing Tom....

Jason got out of bed to see if his parents were still up. They weren't, and it seemed cowardly to wake them over a mere suspicion. He contemplated sleeping on the lounge room sofa but that would have been embarrassing too, so he went back to his bedroom.

Getting to sleep was almost impossible. A strong wind was generating a range of creaks and clunks outside. Every time Jason did manage to doze off, he woke again with a start, imagining he could smell smoke. But his room remained log-free so the smell must have been in his dreams.

●　　●　　●

Jason got up next morning at a bit after eight. In retrospect, it was good that his parents hadn't been up late last night since he was obviously being paranoid about Einstein. Things seemed much less sinister in the light of day.

Jason's parents didn't look up from their respective newspapers as Jason parked himself for breakfast. 'Looks like they're burning off,' said his mother between sips of coffee.

'They must be starting early this year,' replied Mr Saunders.

Jason jumped to his feet and looked out the kitchen window. In the distance, a pall of smoke was blowing across the landscape.

Einstein! thought Jason. *What have you done?*

Chapter 19

Fire-breathing Dragons

Jason cycled flat-out. The wind was blowing the smoke over most of Sapphire Bay, but Jason was pretty sure he knew where to head. The track into the forest might have been okay on a dirt bike but it definitely wasn't okay on his machine. His front wheel dropped into ruts a couple of times and tipped him off. The visibility got worse as he approached the depot; it was like riding through an orange fog. Even though he was puffed, Jason tried not to breathe too deeply because of the smoke.

He pulled up at the clearing that served as a car park. Trees behind the portable office were on fire and the breeze was blowing burning debris onto Mr Wherrett's Range Rover. A fire engine was blasting water at the car and the building even though neither of them seemed to be on fire. The two large trucks in the locked compound had obviously been soaked too.

A hose from the fire engine snaked around the back of the cabin. Jason wheeled his bike along the edge of the car park so he could see where it led. Behind the cabin, three firemen were pointing the hose at a gum tree that was well alight. Lots of bushes were also burning, and glowing embers were flying further into the forest. The firemen seemed tiny compared to the flames they were fighting.

The blaze was surprisingly loud. It crackled and fizzed, and occasionally a burning branch crunched to the ground making Jason jump. The firefighters could be heard yelling instructions to one another, but the details couldn't be discerned over the sound of the fire.

One voice seemed particularly insistent. Jason turned and saw one of the firefighters waving frantically to him. Thinking he was being summoned to help, he took a few paces forward, even though he didn't feel comfortable about getting too close to the inferno. The heat was making him sweat.

'Get out of here!' yelled the firie, holding the hose with one arm and gesturing at Jason with the other.

Jason didn't move. He was overwhelmed by the onslaught of sensations.

'Get lost!' shouted the orange-clad figure.

Jason snapped out of his stupor, turned his bike towards town and took off as fast as the track allowed.

● ● ●

It was a bad day. The morning was punctuated by the sirens of fire engines coming from nearby towns to help. The smoke got thicker and spread across the whole town, resulting in warnings over the radio that people should stay indoors. There was talk of evacuation but nobody seemed to know what was going on. Jason was tempted to cycle to the caravan park so he could spy on the greenies, who were presumably very pleased with themselves.

Except for the lingering smell and yellow haze, it was all over by Sunday. The radio reported that the fire was under control, although it hadn't been possible to contain it before it had spread to a few of the properties that backed onto the forest.

Emma!

Jason tried to call. No answer. He texted 'R u ok?' but that didn't stop him from worrying. He felt a bit responsible because he'd been aware Einstein was about to do something, but how could he have known it would be anything this stupid?

Another morning bike ride was unavoidable. The forest track was blocked by barricades and a police car, but the road to Emma's place was open. Burnt treetops were visible over the roofs of the houses, and smoke was still rising from some of them.

The front of Emma's house looked fine. Many of the greenies were standing on the front lawn talking to Tom, who must have flown back from Tasmania early. Ms Gow was there too, which seemed a bit odd.

Jason didn't want to get too close because he was wasn't popular with the greenies any more, but he had to find out if Emma was okay. Fortunately he managed to catch a glimpse of her through the crowd.

Emma glimpsed Jason's glimpse and beckoned him over. Jason was wary, but Emma seemed insistent. The greenies were busy with Tom so Jason figured it should be safe enough. Emma obviously didn't know that Jason was the source of the accusations against Tom, and if she didn't know, then none of the greenies did. Chandra must have kept Jason's role in discovering Tom's trickery to himself.

If the teacher wanted to take credit for it, that was fine with Jason.

'The front room is trashed,' said Emma quietly. 'Where we watched the rosellas. Remember?'

Jason nodded, not sure what to say or do.

Emma was so up-tight she seemed to be quivering. 'Obviously the loggers did it,' she continued. 'Like when they threw that log at your house.'

Jason had a different theory. He looked across at Einstein and his mates, who were standing a few metres away from the main gathering. Noticing Jason looking at him, Einstein quickly focused his gaze elsewhere.

Jason found it hard to think of a response that wouldn't risk getting him into trouble. 'Do you really think they'd do this?' was the best he could manage.

'They've got it in for Dad. They've started rumours about him. The dragon heard them.'

Before Jason could ask what the rumours were, he was distracted by the arrival of a white Falcon with heavily tinted windows. Mr Wherrett and Roscoe stepped out, as did an older man in a grey suit. All greenie eyes locked onto the new arrivals, who paused at the front of their vehicle. Nobody said a word.

After an awkward delay, the loggers moved slowly forward. 'We heard about what happened to your house,' Mr Wherrett said to Tom. 'It's very regrettable.'

'Told you,' muttered Emma.

Mr Wherrett introduced the grey-suited man he'd arrived with. He was Mr Newell, the owner of the whole logging company Australia-wide. He'd flown in from Sydney by helicopter that morning.

'Did you do this?' asked Gillian.

Mr Newell looked surprised. 'Why would we do it? Our property was damaged too. We think we know who did it, but we're not interested in conflict.'

Roscoe grunted and stared at Einstein.

'I don't think we'll be needing you, Roscoe,' said Mr Wherrett. 'Wait for us by the car.'

Roscoe stood his ground for a while, then dawdled back to the Falcon like a chastised dog. He crossed his arms and sat on the car's bonnet, which creaked under his weight.

'If you're not here to apologise, then why are you here?' Gillian asked Mr Newell.

'To clear the air—so to speak. We're not going to ask for an investigation and we're not going to press charges. We're doing you a big favour. In return, I'm asking you to stop this silliness right now.'

'You're assuming we did it,' said Gillian. 'My people would never do anything like this. We don't resort to bully-boy tactics like throwing logs.'

'I'm not interested in accusations. Just keep your rabble under control.' The boss logger waved an arm towards Tom's house. 'This isn't helping either of us.'

As he was speaking, a smouldering bough from a tree in Tom's back yard crashed to the ground.

'It isn't helping the forest, either,' added Mr Wherrett. 'Neither of us wants burnt trees.'

●　　●　　●

The weekend had been one drama after another. Jason sat at his desk on Sunday afternoon trying to concentrate on a geography assignment, but it wasn't happening. Gillian's arrival was a surprising but welcome distraction.

'I've been trying to make sense of what happened to Tom,' she said, lowering herself into a recliner in the lounge room. 'He doesn't deserve this.'

Jason kept his mouth shut, so Gillian continued. 'I keep hearing about a rumour against Tom. Tom's partner seems to know all about it but she won't tell me what's going on. When I wouldn't give up, she said I should speak to you.'

'I don't know what she's talking about,' replied Jason. 'I've never met her.'

'Are you sure? She works at your school. She teaches English, I think.'

'Ms Gow!'

That made sense. Ms Gow, AKA 'the dragon', must have told Tom about Jason's essay, but didn't let on that it was Jason's. Tom will have told Einstein, who assumed the loggers were behind it, so he went ahead with his plan.

'So you *do* know her,' said Gillian. 'Look, Jason, this is out of control. If you're in on the secret, you have to tell me. Thousands of dollars' damage has been done to the home of an innocent man.'

Jason knew she was right, at least about things being out of control. He was also painfully aware he'd taken too long to show his work to someone who could sort it out properly. He retrieved his essay from his room and handed it to the lawyer.

Maybe it was just the sun setting through the smoky sky, but Gillian's face seemed to get redder with every page she turned. When she'd finished, she placed the document on the coffee table and sat staring out the window. Her expressionless face gave no clue about whether she believed what she'd read, or whether Jason had just got himself even further off-side with her.

'I can understand why the loggers did it,' she said finally.

Jason wanted to spill his guts over his suspicion about Einstein but he didn't have any real evidence. And Gillian was always on about evidence. Dobbing on Einstein would have been a bad plan anyway, since Einstein was obviously not one to miss an opportunity for revenge— even when it was misguided.

'Will QAP think of something else to focus on, since there aren't any quolls?' asked Jason, hoping to distract Gillian from thinking about who started the fire.

'If the loggers knew about this,' said the lawyer, tapping a finger on Jason's essay, 'why didn't they just tell everyone what Tom was doing?'

'I never showed it to them. I only showed it to teachers at school.'

'But if the loggers didn't know about Tom, why did they start the fire?'

Jason shrugged. 'Does Tom need to know it was me who dobbed him in?'

'He'll find out sooner or later. Don't worry, if he so much as talks to you about this, I'll get him locked up within the hour.'

Gillian left for Tom's place with a fierce expression on her face. Jason thought about cycling back there to watch the fireworks but realised it wouldn't be safe. The confrontation was bound to be as intense as the bushfire.

Despite the discomfort of knowing he'd just got Tom into major trouble, Jason was relieved his discovery was finally going to be dealt with. With the right evidence, people believed him. Maybe he could make a difference after all. Now, the forest will get the help it needed.

Unfortunately, every silver lining has a cloud. Emma, the dragon's step-daughter, would be breathing fire. He'd be dead by Monday recess at the latest. Perhaps, after incinerating him, his ex-nearly-sort-of-girlfriend would be willing to add his ashes to the forest. Jason's final favour to the trees would be as fertiliser.

Chapter 20

Crows in the Forest

Breakfast was awkward on Monday morning. Jason's parents congratulated him on his work to expose Tom, although it was obvious Mr Saunders would have preferred that it hadn't happened. Every setback for the greenies made it more likely that he'd have to sack people at his factory, like Bull's mum. But numbers can't lie: Tom did it, and that was that.

The fire was big news. It made the front page of the *Sapphire Sentinel*, and pictures of burnt houses extended for several pages into the paper. There were two pictures of the back of Emma's place, showing a gaping hole where the wall of windows used to be. It was pretty sickening. The loggers' depot hadn't been damaged much at all because the wind had blown the flames away from it. Trust Einstein to stuff it up.

The paper said the fire had started near the loggers' depot. Jason hoped that would stop the greenies from accusing the loggers of starting it. But the fire investigators didn't know *how* it started, or *why*. The newspaper

183

mentioned the battle between the greenies and the loggers, and even named Jason as being involved. But Jason wasn't worried about getting more bad publicity because he had a more immediate problem.

•　　•　　•

Jason didn't even manage to get to his first class before being hunted down by Emma.

'Everyone hates my Dad now and he won't tell me why. He said you did it to him because he stopped you from coming over.'

Jason ferreted through his bag for his English folder and took out his essay. He suddenly realised he should have made a photocopy of it since it was unlikely he'd get the original back in one piece. Not that it really mattered; the only thing he couldn't reprint was Ms Gow's comment. And she was obviously biased, so her opinion didn't count for much.

Emma snatched the essay out of Jason's hand and examined it. Jason was careful to stand out of reach of her gangly arms.

After a couple of minutes, Emma slammed the assignment down on the desk in front of her. 'How *could* he?' she demanded.

Jason couldn't respond straight away because he wasn't prepared for that kind of reaction. Even though Emma probably wasn't expecting an answer, it seemed like a good opportunity to try to calm her down. 'He was probably doing it for you, a bit. You like the birds in the forest.'

'I never asked him to cheat. I'll bet he was doing it for the dragon's beloved bed-and-breakfast. I'm glad it's burnt.'

'Oh yeah. Why didn't you tell me Ms Gow was your step-mother?'

'Would you want everyone to know if your mother was a teacher here? Anyway, it was kinda funny, you trashing her in front of me.' Emma managed half a smile, but it faded quickly.

'You're the one who calls her the dragon. She must have told your dad about this,' said Jason as he retrieved his assignment.

'I can see why everyone's saying Dad got what he deserved. I hate him for this.'

Jason hadn't anticipated being responsible for wrecking Emma's relationship with her father. He quietly apologised.

'You didn't do anything wrong,' replied Emma. 'Not like my father. It's like I don't have any parents at all now.'

• • •

After school on Tuesday, Jason hit the shops to buy Emma a gift to say sorry about her dad and thanks for believing him. As he walked across the car park, he noticed Einstein's dinged-up ute straddling two spaces. Einstein wasn't in it, so Jason accelerated his pace to get past it as quickly as possible. But the sight of a log in the back of the ute made him stop.

What was it about the log? There was nothing strange about having one in the back of a ute. Einstein was probably going to use it for a campfire or barbecue at the caravan park. Jason stared at it for a while. It had been sawn in half along its length; its face had saw marks at two distinct angles.

Just like the one that had been thrown through his bedroom window!

Jason was stunned. Einstein did that? Why? Weren't they on the same side at the time?

'What are you looking at?' said a voice behind him.

Jason swung around. Einstein was only a few metres away, and Tom was with him. Until last week, Jason could have counted on Tom to protect him from Einstein, but not any more.

Einstein looked at the log, then back at Jason. 'Figured it out, have you?'

Jason nodded slowly. Einstein was standing so close that Jason could smell his BO.

'What?' asked Tom.

'Brilliant plan, eh?' said Einstein. 'You needed revving up. So did them other wimps.'

Tom looked bewildered. 'What?' he repeated.

Einstein ignored Tom and moved even closer to Jason. 'Serves you right too, for getting me in the shit with the bloody lawyer. Just because I was on TV.'

'Will someone *please* tell me what's going on?' begged Tom.

Jason desperately wanted to clue Tom in but didn't dare say anything with Einstein in his face. It required all his courage to take his eyes off Einstein so he could focus on the log.

Tom followed Jason's gaze and studied the log for a few seconds, then suddenly looked back at Einstein. '*You* did that? *You* attacked Jason's house?'

'You're such a wuss,' said Einstein wearily. 'I knew you wouldn't be in it.'

Tom stared aghast at Einstein, who just looked nonchalantly back. Jason took the opportunity to drift gradually out of Einstein's reach.

'Gillian was right to get me to babysit you,' said Tom eventually.

Einstein smirked. 'Not doing a very good job then, are you? Like I said, you're a wuss. Although I *am* impressed about that quoll shit thing.'

'I didn't do that!' protested Tom, who was obviously trying not to even look at Jason. 'How many times do I have to tell you?'

'It would've been good if you'd got away with it—'

'I didn't bloody do it!'

'—but you got caught so you've buggered it up for all of us.'

Jason backed further away as the two greenies argued. They heaved their purchases into the back of the ute and drove off, seemingly forgetting about Jason. That didn't disappoint him in the slightest.

• • •

It didn't take long for the media to find out what Tom had done. It was on the TV news on Wednesday night. The background image to the segment said 'QUOLLGATE'; Mr Saunders reckoned that sounded like a toothpaste for marsupials.

A reporter had accosted Gillian near the entrance to the caravan park and accused her of lying about the quolls.

'We did make some mistakes, but my group firmly believes—'

'Your group is called QAP, isn't it?'

Gillian nodded glumly.

'Yes, but you need to look at the arguments—'

'How can we trust the arguments if we can't trust the people making them? Your members falsified evidence so they could make more money.'

'One of our ex-members, yes. But most of us have given up a lot to try to protect—'

'Did you really call yourselves QAP?' asked Mr Saunders.

Now it was Jason's turn to nod glumly. 'I'm not one of them now, though.'

'Looks like they QAPed in their own nest.'

Perhaps that name wasn't such a great choice after all, thought Jason.

The TV interview went on for a while longer, with Gillian trying to raise other issues but the reporter always bringing it back to Tom's lies. At one point, Gillian said there wasn't any evidence that thinning was actually good for the forest, but the reporter reminded her about Jason's thinning spreadsheet: 'Your own mascot came out in favour of thinning!'

Gillian could only nod again.

After the interview, the reporter mentioned the fire and hinted that the greenies could have started it. She even implied that Mr Lindsay could have something to do with the greenies because of his connection with Jason.

'Mr Lindsay won't like that,' said Jason's mother.

•　　•　　•

Mrs Saunders was right. Jason was about to cycle down to see Gillian after school on Thursday when there was a phone call from the PM. Not surprisingly, he didn't have a clue what was going on. He asked if Jason knew anything about the fire and Jason said he didn't, which was sort-of true because he didn't have any proof. Mr Lindsay's main concern seemed to be for Jason not to do anything silly, probably because the media would link it back to him.

After reassuring the PM, Jason struck out for Gillian's. As he knocked on the cabin door, he realised her pot plant wasn't there any more. Gillian opened the door, revealing several open suitcases.

'You're leaving?' asked Jason.

'Most of us are,' replied the lawyer, folding a blouse. 'We can't win this. Not now.'

Jason sat down and kicked at the nearest table leg. 'I came to apologise. I'm sorry about Tom.'

Gillian looked up in surprise. 'You didn't do anything wrong! Tom did, and you were right to point out his lies.' She dumped a stack of blouses into the nearest suitcase with unnecessary force. 'That greedy liar has done more to destroy our cause than the loggers ever could have.'

• • •

Jason shot out of school as quickly as possible on Friday afternoon so he could make it for the start of Mr Wherrett's next press conference. The logger had scheduled the event for late in the day just so Jason could be there. Jason was looking forward to it because, if the loggers announced what he expected them to, it would be like claiming victory. A victory he'd contributed to in more ways than one. And since Mr Wherrett didn't know that Jason had anything to do with exposing Tom, there'd be no reason for him to be mentioned so he could just sit back and watch.

He got to the forest car park with a couple of minutes to spare. There were about a dozen reporters' cars there, including a specky red Nissan 370Z Roadster. Clearly there was good money to be made in reporting.

Jason took up a vantage point on a wooden fence well away from the audience. It was a fine spring afternoon, and the forest resounded with the squawks of parrots getting busy for nesting season. Emma would have loved it.

Mr Newell, the boss of the logging company, had obviously made the trip down from Sydney for the occasion. However, when it was time to start the conference, he let Mr Wherrett do the talking: 'Australian Forestry Industries is happy to announce that the government has given us the green light to resume thinning operations in Sapphire State Forest. We're relieved that we'll be able to restore the forest to a sustainable state without impacting on any endangered species. We don't feel any ill will towards the environmentalists who've questioned this project, and we hope to work closely with environmentally-minded locals as the task to maintain the forest gets into top gear.'

Mr Wherrett looked across to Jason and waved an arm in his direction. 'I know he'll hate me for saying this, but our relationship with Jason Saunders is a perfect example.'

Jason felt like he was turning as red as the Roadster. A few of the reporters snapped pictures of him while Mr Wherrett carried on. 'Last time we were here, I showed you Jason's work confirming that thinning the forest will be good for it. Now I can show you how he worked out that there aren't any quolls here.'

Like last time, Mr Wherrett held up some big printouts from Jason's computer work. And like last time, Jason had no idea where the logger got his information from.

After a few questions from the audience, the conference was over and the reporters headed for their cars. Jason tried to predict which one of them owned the 370Z, but after they'd all left, the sports car remained.

Mr Wherrett walked over to Jason. 'Sorry to embarrass you like that, but I just had to acknowledge your brilliant work. We couldn't have done this properly if you hadn't figured out what Tom Johnson was up to.'

'What's going to happen to him?'

'The police wanted us to press charges. They were quite insistent, actually. But we're not going to.'

'Why not?'

'We're not lawyers. We just want to fix this place up.' Mr Wherrett waved an arm at the gums around them.

Jason nodded towards the Roadster. 'Whose car?'

'Mine,' replied the logger proudly. 'And no, you can't take it for a spin.'

'I thought the beaten-up Range Rover was yours.'

'Company car. Now *that* I would have let you drive.'

Mr Wherrett excused himself and went to talk to the other loggers. The sun on Jason's back was pleasantly warm, as was the feeling that he'd helped Mr Wherrett and the forest. Maybe he could get a job with Australian Forestry Industries when he finished school. Or maybe he could follow in Mr Lindsay's footsteps and become a politician. After all, if he could convince Emma that her beloved father was a cheat, he could convince anyone of anything.

A crimson rosella squawked noisily between the trees. Jason had never paid much attention to birds before, but found himself watching them more often since he'd been hanging out with Emma. She was the only good thing to have come out of the greenies' campaign.

Things had sort-of worked out backwards for the greenies. They were the ones who'd dragged Jason into this, and they were expecting him to help get rid of the loggers. But their plan backfired since he exposed what they were up to. Good riddance to them.

'Young man, I understand I owe you a debt of gratitude.'

Jason dropped his focus from the treetops and saw Mr Newell standing before him. 'That's okay,' he replied.

It was just as well Mr Newell hadn't done the talking at the press conference because he was a windbag. He crapped on about how his company always did the right thing and how thinning was so great, even though he knew Jason had worked that out for himself.

It didn't help that Mr Wherrett was joking loudly with the other loggers a few metres away. Jason tried to tune in to their conversation since it was obviously more entertaining than Mr Newell.

'They've been dis*quoll*ified,' said one of the loggers. The others laughed.

'—for s*quoll*id behaviour,' added someone else. More laughter.

Mr Wherrett turned to Roscoe and said, 'I told you my project *quoll*ifications would be good enough.'

Roscoe was the only one not smiling. 'I still think this ain't proper.'

'Leave the thinking to me,' replied Mr Wherrett. That didn't make Roscoe look any happier.

'Project quollifications' sounded vaguely familiar, but Jason couldn't remember where he'd heard it before. It was hard to concentrate with Mr Newell blabbing away in front of him. Even so, something didn't seem right.

Jason said as little as possible to Mr Newell in the hope he'd go away. After a few more minutes of pointless advertising, he did. Jason jumped straight on his bike and rocketed down to the caravan park on the off-chance Gillian hadn't left yet.

She hadn't. 'You can't go!' blurted Jason between pants.

'You never cease to surprise me, Jason,' said the lawyer. 'Why can't I go?'

'I don't know.' Realising that didn't sound terribly compelling, he added, 'I've just heard, um, funny things from the loggers.'

'What things?'

'I don't know.' That phrase again. 'Something about their qualifications, maybe.'

Gillian gave Jason a you-can-do-better-than-that look, which he was more than familiar with from school. 'If you know something, you'd better come out with it.'

'But, um, I want to get evidence. You said we had to have evidence.'

'Then get it. And get it legally, or it doesn't count.'

'Will you wait?'

Gillian sat down wearily on her bed. 'How serious are you?'

Jason's first reaction was to say *I don't know* but he managed to catch himself in time. 'Very. Totally.'

The lawyer eyed him suspiciously, while Jason tried to look twelve times more confident than he felt.

'Okay,' said Gillian in a resigned tone. 'But this had better be good.'

Chapter 21

A Fishy Folder

Jason woke early on Saturday with a hunch about 'quollifications'. Even though it was cold, he got up and started his laptop.

Now where was it? It had been three weeks since he'd dredged through the computer's folders looking for numbers for his thinning spreadsheet. Because so much had happened since then, it seemed like six months.

A quick skim didn't find anything, so he got Windows to do a search for `quollifications`. After thinking about it for a while, the operating system responded with `No items match your search`. Jason tried all the spelling variations he could think of, but always scored the same result.

He was getting seriously cold by now. He contemplated accidentally making a bit of noise to wake his father so they could get the fire going, but then he'd have to put up with the stinge winging about the price of firewood. It was less hassle to just use the laptop in bed.

Since Windows wasn't going to co-operate and find `quollifications` on its own, there seemed to be no option but to look in every folder. Jason started scanning. Fortunately, `\\AFI` jumped out at him almost immediately. AFI probably stood for Australian Forestry Industries. Jason now remembered seeing Mr Wherrett's personal stuff in `\\AFI`; things like `coarses` and `experiance`.

But double-clicking on `\\AFI` only brought up `Windows cannot access this folder.` That didn't happen before. Jason tried three times. He checked the network connection and tried once more. No go. The loggers must have changed the settings so he couldn't get into that folder.

Mr Wherrett would be able to access it, though. After all, it was his stuff. Jason tried to log into his computer using Mr Wherrett's account, but the user name on his computer was locked to `saunders_jason`.

It was only reasonable for the loggers to block people from getting into `\\AFI` since it was their private info. But it was hard not to be suspicious.

•   •   •

On Monday evening, Jason's father came home from work in an unusually good mood. 'God bless those loggers,' he said.

Mr Saunders' change of heart was triggered by a jump in sales to the local takeaway shops. Now that the thinning project was getting close to starting, more and more loggers were flooding into town—and they were obviously voracious fish-and-chip eaters. Logging didn't seem to be bad for business after all. Maybe Bull's mother wouldn't need to be sacked now, and there was even a chance of Predator repairs.

'Weren't the greenies eating your stuff?' asked Jason. 'They're going soon.'

Mr Saunders blew a raspberry. 'Those dole bludgers can't afford good fish. I'll bet most of them are vegetarians, anyway.'

Until a few days ago, Jason would have been elated that his father had changed his mind about logging. Now he wasn't so sure. Just when everything seemed to be sorted out, the loggers had to go all weird. If he found out anything that got them kicked out of town—something to do with 'quollifications', for instance—then he'd be back where he started: off-side with Dad, hiding from Bull, and a dead Predator.

Even if something strange was going on, that didn't change the fact that thinning was good for the forest. Jason tried to convince himself he should just leave the loggers to do their thing. Let it go. Let it go.

But his brain wouldn't. Tom and Emma were suffering, and something didn't add up. There wasn't much to go on: the only clues were the loggers' bad jokes, Mr Wherrett's 'quollifications', and a private folder on the loggers' computer network.

Of course, that folder was only private because Jason's computer wouldn't accept Mr Wherrett's log-in details. He could probably get into the folder if he could use a computer that would accept Mr Wherrett's account details.

And he knew where he could find such a computer.

Chapter 22

Search for the Smoking Pun

Jason excused himself after dinner on Friday. 'Going to get some info from Mr Wherrett,' he told his parents, which was a bit true but also a bit misleading. Mr Saunders, now utterly pro-logger, waved approvingly.

The forest track was too treacherous to attempt with a bicycle at night, so walking was the only option. Jason had hoped he wouldn't need to use his torch but the light from the cloud-filtered sliver of moon didn't cut it.

After about fifteen minutes, the outline of the demountable came into view. Jason was slightly disappointed it was deserted because that deprived him of an excuse to turn around and go home. He knew what he was doing was risky and wrong. At least, if everything went well, he'd be leaving the place exactly as he found it.

He took out his student card and ran it up the gap in the cabin door. When it hit an obstruction, he manoeuvred it around as he'd seen Emma do at her house. He could feel the latch, but no amount of pushing or jiggling would move it.

Jason had considered inviting Emma to come with him tonight, just in case this happened. He'd even worked out how to justify it to her: if it was okay for her to commit break-ins, why couldn't he? But she'd want to know what he was looking for, and he didn't even know that himself. It wasn't likely to be home-cooked biscuits, though.

He gave up on the door. Maybe Emma's trick would work on a window. The cabin only had one window, but fortunately it was a sliding window.

Or it would have been a sliding window if Jason had been able to weave his student card around the contours in its frame. The card didn't want to know about it. It kept bending instead of going where it was supposed to.

Jason pushed harder and harder, expecting the card to snap at any moment.

Then, partial success: the card squeezed into the gap— and stayed there. Jason couldn't get it any further in, but it wouldn't go in any other direction either. He gripped it with both hands and tugged. Finally the card came free and fluttered over his shoulder into the darkness.

Jason muttered something his mother wouldn't have approved of, and shone the torch towards the card's probable landing site. Not seeing it, he started raking through the leaves and ashes on the ground with his shoe.

Footsteps!

Definitely. Crunching through the ashes, and not far away. Jason fumbled as he tried to turn the torch off and it joined the student card somewhere on the ground. The impact extinguished the light. And halted the footsteps.

The intruder's torch beam disappeared after a second. The only sound was the occasional rustle of leaves in the forest. Jason's first instinct was to try to find his torch, but the new arrival could spotlight him at any instant. The torch was probably broken anyway. Abandoning his lost items, he groped for the cabin behind him, then slunk around behind it.

The nocturnal bushwalker's torch came on again and the footsteps resumed, albeit slower. Jason bent down and looked under the demountable. The light beam was just about up to the building when its carrier tripped and fell to the ground.

'What the…?' exclaimed an annoyed male voice that sounded familiar, although Jason couldn't quite identify it.

The figure got back to his feet, then picked up Jason's torch—and his student card.

'Sanders,' mumbled the voice.

Jason breathed with relief. He really didn't want to be traced to the loggers' depot after dark. Who was this annoying visitor? Who in their right mind would be walking here at this time of day?

'No, *Saunders*. Jason Saunders.'

Bugger. Now there'd be some explaining to do.

Worse, Jason recognised the voice this time. It wasn't anyone in their right mind. It was Einstein. The very person you wouldn't want to meet on your own in the middle of a forest at night.

It wasn't hard to guess why he was here. He was bound to be planning to finish what he tried to do two weeks ago. Einstein always did his dirty work on Friday nights, and Tom was due to be away again this weekend. Jason kicked himself for picking the worst possible time to mount his own mission. Perhaps he was subconsciously copying Einstein. What a great role model.

Jason watched Einstein's legs approach the front of the cabin. Suddenly the legs were accompanied by an arm and a head, as the dimwit bent down to look under the demountable. 'You can come out now, Saunders,' he said, flashing his torch around.

Jason considered running into the forest, but since Einstein had the only source of illumination, the gronk would have had no difficulty catching him.

The circle of light swept over Jason's shoes, then backtracked and stayed there. 'Come on. I'm not gunna kill ya. Probably.'

Jason emerged sheepishly, and Einstein was kind enough to drop his torch's beam from Jason's face after a while. They looked at each other in the dim glow that reflected off the side of the cabin. Eventually, Einstein bent down and placed a jerrycan on the ground.

'Petrol?' asked Jason.

'Wouldn't have needed it if you hadn't pranged your car.'

Jason looked mystified.

'Logs woulda been better but they was too heavy to lug. Petrol burns too quick, and the stupid building's made of steel.'

Jason thought better than to correct Einstein's metallurgy by pointing out that it was aluminium.

'So it's your fault the forest got torched,' added Einstein. 'And your girlfriend's house.'

Jason blinked. Was Einstein trying to pass the blame for the fire that he himself had lit?

The light brightened for a moment. Jason and Einstein looked back along the track.

There it was again: headlights filtering through bush. After another flash, an engine became audible. Jason scurried around the back of the cabin again, but Einstein just stayed put.

The vehicle stopped in front of the building. A car door opened and closed.

'I suspected as much.' It was Tom's voice.

'You're supposed to be in Tassie,' said Einstein.

'You lit the fire, didn't you? And you were about to do it again.' A boot tapped the jerrycan. 'I ought to kill you for what you did to my house.'

'Not a good idea when there's a witness. Unless you're gunna kill Saunders, too.'

Thanks, Einstein, thought Jason. There was no point hiding any more so he emerged from behind the cabin.

'You were going to help this moron commit arson?' asked Tom incredulously. 'But you're a raging logger now! You sure as hell shafted me.'

'Your house was just an accident,' said Einstein. 'Of course *you've* never had an accident, like getting sprung for that animal crap thing.'

'I didn't bloody do that!' Tom looked like he was about to take a swing at Einstein, but then dropped his shoulders. 'I give up. Nobody's ever going to believe me. Even my daughter hates me.'

'Actually, that's why I came here,' said Jason.

Tom looked at Jason quizzically, but Einstein just picked up his jerrycan. 'I came here to torch this place. So are youse gunna let me stop the logging, or what?'

'You don't have to trash stuff to stop the logging,' said Jason.

Tom hadn't taken his eyes off Jason. 'I'm not supposed to talk to you, but what do you know, Jason?'

'Nothing. But there might be stuff on their computer. Evidence.'

'Gee, that sounds interesting,' said Einstein. 'Like hell it does.'

'Evidence about me?' asked Tom.

Jason didn't answer.

'Evidence about me?' repeated Tom.

'Don't keep asking me stuff. I might be wrong. I always seem to be wrong.'

'Yeah, well, you were wrong about me. But you shouldn't do this. Tell me what you're looking for and I'll find it.'

'Do you know how to hack into a computer?' asked Jason. 'Anyway, if there's going to break-in, it doesn't make any difference who does it.'

Tom didn't look convinced, so Jason tried a different tack. 'Like you said, I'm a raging logger now. So it's okay for me to go in and look at logger stuff.'

'I'll do it,' offered Einstein.

Tom grunted, then walked over to his X-Trail. He returned with a crowbar which he inserted into the gap beside the cabin's door. Gentle prying flexed the door but didn't open it. He relocated the lever and tried again.

'Give me that,' demanded Einstein, which was redundant since he'd already snatched the bar out of Tom's hands. He swung it at the window and smashed it. Reaching inside, he unlocked the door.

Jason crunched carefully across the broken glass by torchlight. After checking Mr Wherrett's computer for shards of glass, he pressed its power button.

Bright light instantly flooded the room. Jason's already-pounding heart pounded harder again. What had he done wrong? Was this some sort of security system? He quickly pressed the power button again, but the light remained.

'Turn that off!' said Tom shrilly.

'Okay, okay,' replied Einstein. He flicked the demountable's lights off again.

Jason resumed breathing, and restarted the computer. Windows seemed to take forever to load. How come computers always started more slowly when you needed them in a hurry?

Finally the log-in window popped up. Already things looked more promising than on Jason's laptop, since the user name area was blank. Jason typed wherrett_, then stopped.

Tom looked worried. 'Can't you log on?'

'Maybe only loggers can log on,' suggested Einstein, from his position at the door. 'Greenies have to green on.'

Jason ignored Einstein's attempt at humour. 'What's Mr Wherrett's first name?'

'How would I know?' said Tom. 'He's your friend, not mine.'

They looked on the desk for any paperwork with Mr Wherrett's name on it, but all they could find was a memo marked 'F. Wherrett'. That was a start, but not enough.

'We'll have to guess,' said Tom. 'Try "Frank".'

Jason winced. 'We only get three goes. After that, it locks us out.'

'I reckon it's something gay,' said Einstein. 'Flowers, or something.'

'That's not helpful, Einstein,' replied Tom. 'You just keep an eye out for security patrols.'

But Einstein's comment triggered a reaction in Jason's brain. 'No, he's right. Flowers … floral … Florian!' Jason typed that in, followed by the password he'd managed to notice when Mr Wherrett had set up his laptop. Of course, that was a while ago; if the logger was strict about security, he'd have changed it since then.

But he hadn't. The computer swallowed the log-in details, and icons started popping onto the desktop. As soon as it settled down, Jason looked for the AFI folder.

It was there.

Better yet, when Jason double-clicked on it, the folder opened to reveal the sub-folders he'd seen before: FW, SaffireForrest—and ProjectQuollifications.

' "SaffireForrest",' said Tom. 'It's bound to be in there, the stuff about me.'

But Jason double-clicked on ProjectQuollifications. After skimming the list of files that appeared, he opened one called Plan.doc.

Tom started reading aloud: ' "For the Saffire Forrest project to succede, we must avoid close scrutiny. Enviromental groups are the biggest threat." '

'This bloke can't spell for peanuts,' commented Tom. 'What an amateur.'

'No, he's just bad at spelling,' said Jason. 'He knows a lot about—'

'Rubbish. Look down here.' Tom tapped on the screen. 'He's talking about making trips to "pick up crap". A professional wouldn't say "crap" in an official document. You'd say "materials" or "supplies".'

'Not if you actually mean it.' Jason pointed to a paragraph further down the document.

Tom read it to himself. 'Those arseholes!'

'What?' asked Einstein, who was still keeping watch.

'Wherrett's mob knew about my trips to Tasmania,' said Tom. 'One of them went down there as well, to collect quoll droppings. They put it in the forest for me to find. They even knew where I walked!'

Einstein thought about that. 'So you didn't put it there yourself? Shame. I thought that was pretty cool. Except you got caught.'

'But I wasn't really caught, was I? I was framed. I was *used*.'

'You're not the only one,' said Jason, who'd been reading further ahead. 'Listen to this: "To avoid being seen to be in conflict with enviro-mental groups, we will use a third party to expose them".'

'I don't get it,' said Tom.

'I'm the "third party". They used me to discover that you were planting the poo. Although you actually weren't.'

'This is going straight to the cops,' said Tom, flicking the monitor.

Jason screwed up his face. 'What did they actually do wrong?'

'They framed me!'

'All they did was spread some manure around. That's not illegal—but breaking in here is. And Gillian said evidence doesn't count if you don't get it legally.'

Tom flopped down into Mr Wherrett's chair. 'But we have to do *something*.'

'I'll get a copy of this for now. We can work out what to do with it later.' Jason tried to pull a memory stick from his pocket but it didn't want to come. When it finally did, it flicked out and fell to the floor a couple of metres away.

While Einstein illuminated the area, Jason groped around for the device. The distant torchlight wasn't really up to the job and he cut himself on a splinter of glass. The throbbing finger went straight into his mouth.

'You don't need your memory stick,' said Tom. 'Just leave it.'

'I can't. It's got my schoolwork on it. They'd work out it was mine.'

Tom managed to find the device and handed it to Jason. 'Is that blood?' he asked.

Jason held up his cut finger.

'Ouch. There's blood on the floor, too. I hope they don't trace that to you.'

Jason hadn't thought about that. 'I'll wipe it up before we go.' He went to insert his memory stick into the computer but Tom stopped him.

'You don't need to do that,' said Tom. 'While you were grovelling around on the floor, I emailed the file to each of us. See, you're not the only one who knows about computers.'

Jason looked at Tom for signs he was kidding. 'Do you know about server logs?'

'Surfer logs?' echoed Einstein. 'They're making surfboards out of logs? So what if they are?'

'*Server* logs. Computer records about emails and stuff. The loggers will be able to see who the email was sent to.'

Tom bit his lower lip. 'Can you hide them, or something?'

The keyboard suddenly got darker as Einstein turned off his torch. 'Car.'

By the light of the screen, Jason started the computer's shutdown process and watched as each program finalised its activity.

'We haven't got time for that,' said Tom.

'If you don't shut down a computer properly, it can screw up the file system.'

'Tough. This guy's the enemy.' Tom jabbed the computer's power button, and they scrambled out of the cabin while silhouettes cast by the approaching headlights danced around the walls.

The trio piled into Tom's X-Trail. Using only parking lights for visibility, Tom coaxed the 4WD further along the track into the forest. After going around a bend, he did a three-point turn, then turned off the ignition and switched off the lights.

The approaching beams swung off to the side then disappeared. A car door slammed.

The X-Trail's engine roared to life and its driving lights flashed on, causing Jason to squint. They lurched forward and bounced past the depot as fast as the conditions allowed. Jason tried to see who'd arrived there but it was too dark.

As they rallied out of the forest, Jason looked out the rear window to see if they were being chased, but they made it to the bitumen with no sign of the other car. They'd gotten away with it—as long as the loggers didn't trace the email Tom had sent. Or Jason's blood. Or Einstein's jerrycan. Or probably a million other things.

Assuming Tom hadn't stuffed up sending the email, evidence of the loggers' treachery would be waiting in Jason's email inbox. But it was illegal evidence. What to do with it?

Chapter 23

Quollateral Damage

'Are you sure they don't know who you are?' asked Jason.

Tom nodded. 'Just like I've been sure every other time you've asked me that.'

Jason still wasn't convinced. Tom was desperate to clear his name and had insisted on giving `Plan.doc` to a reporter anonymously. Jason would have preferred not to do anything until he'd had a chance to study the document more closely, but he had to admit Tom had more at stake. That was on Tuesday. Ever since, Jason had been expecting a call from Mr Wherrett, or a visit from Roscoe, saying they'd worked out he was responsible for swiping the file. Fortunately that hadn't happened, not even after the story appeared in the *Sapphire Sentinel* on Thursday.

But now it was Friday afternoon, and the start of school holidays. The remaining QAPers were gathering around Gillian's cabin because there was going to be a story on the TV news about the loggers framing Tom. Jason was uncomfortable about being there because many of the greenies still thought he was a traitor, even though

Tom had told them Jason was simply being used by the loggers. Jason's popularity would have skyrocketed if he and Tom had been willing to reveal it was Jason who discovered the loggers' plan, but then everyone would have known it was them who did the break-in.

Jason was looking forward to catching up with Emma at the gathering. He hadn't seen her all week and was bursting to see how relieved she was now he'd proved her father wasn't a cheat after all. Being Tom's hero was one thing; being Emma's hero was untold better.

Emma hadn't arrived yet so Jason hung around with Tom, even though the man wouldn't shut up about what Jason had done. 'Let me thank you again for getting me out of this mess,' he said under his breath.

'But I'm the one who accused you!'

'You couldn't have done anything else, given the info you had. And if you hadn't done it, the loggers would have made sure someone else did.'

Jason grunted. Tom was right, but he still felt a bit dirty because of his inadvertent role in Project Quollifications.

Emma appeared around the side of the canvas annex and dumped her school bag in the corner. Although Jason was sure she'd seen where he and Tom were, she didn't come over. Maybe she assumed their conversation was private. Jason gave her a wave, but she still stayed put.

'Mind if I talk to Emma?' Jason asked Tom.

'Good luck. She's in a strange mood at the moment.'

Tom was right. Emma stared straight into Jason's face. She never did that. 'How *could* you?' she demanded with such vehemence that Jason took a step back.

'What?'

'You accused my father of cheating and you were *wrong!*'

'But I— but it's sorted it out now. Didn't you hear?'

'I don't care. You made me hate him for a while, because you made a mistake.'

Jason didn't know what to say. Fortunately, he didn't have to say anything straight away because Gillian called for silence, then turned up the volume on the portable TV. Tom beckoned Jason over to get a better view.

Fortunately Tom seemed to be right that the media didn't know who was responsible for handing over `Plan.doc`. They just said it was 'an anonymous informant'. After the reporter had read out parts of the document, Mr Wherrett's boss, Mr Newell, came on:

Australian Forestry Industries does not condone this type of activity. We'll be conducting an investigation to see if there's any truth to the allegations. That won't be easy because we don't know where this mysterious document came from, although we do wish to discuss the matter with the so-called Quoll Action Party.

'That wasn't us!' said Gillian, as though Mr Newell could hear her through the TV. 'It could have been leaked by one of your own people. Or a hacker could have broken into your computer.'

Tom was watching the TV with an expressionless face, but Einstein was grinning like an idiot.

Mr Newell continued:

'I'd like to take this opportunity to reassure your viewers that this will have no effect on the Sapphire State Forest thinning project.'

213

Incredulous shouts and boos drowned out the TV. Einstein threw a beer can at the screen, which didn't impress Gillian very much.

'How can they still do that?' asked Jason.

'As far as they're concerned, thinning is still a good idea,' replied Tom. 'You said so yourself.'

Gillian held up her hand for silence and pointed at the TV.

If the accusation against Australian Forestry Industries turns out to be true, we will certainly offer a full apology to Mr Johnson for any inconvenience caused.

'*Inconvenience!*' muttered Tom. 'My daughter hated me for it.'

'And now she hates me,' replied Jason. Emma's reaction had totally taken the high out of the victory over the loggers. The basic problem, once again, was that Jason had made claims that turned out to be wrong. Was there *ever* a right time to speak up about anything? No matter how long you waited, no matter how careful you were, you could still be mistaken.

And some people won't forgive you for that.

•　　•　　•

That evening, Jason tried to forget about Emma, and the whole loggers-versus-greenies thing, by watching a stupid zombie movie on TV. A phone call had taken Mrs Saunders into the kitchen. After about ten minutes, she returned and beckoned to Jason. 'It's Mr Lindsay.'

Jason rolled his eyes. The man was paranoid. After the media managed to bring up his name in their coverage of the fire, it was inevitable the PM would have his knickers in a knot about the latest news story. It was only a matter of time before someone accused him of organising the break-in. Obviously the politician wanted to hear that Jason had nothing to do with it.

'The greenies were going to do something to the depot anyway,' said Jason. 'I'm only one small person, so it doesn't make any difference whether I was involved or not.' *That ought to shut him up*, thought Jason, since it was the same argument the PM had used to wimp out of the Rotterdam emission control agreement.

'Everyone is just one person, but we all have to do the right thing. We all influence the people around us.'

Jason couldn't believe his ears. How could the PM say that? 'I heard that other countries have decided to trash the environment now that you've stopped having emission controls.'

It took the PM a while to respond. 'I honestly wish we could do more about climate change, but that's a separate issue.'

The man just didn't get it. There didn't seem to be any point trying to explain, and Jason figured he'd better not say anything more. His mother would be furious if she found out he'd been rude to the PM. Things were tense enough at home as it was, since he'd managed to infuriate the loggers and then the greenies. And now he'd upset the loggers again, but at least they didn't know it was him.

Unfortunately, Jason suspected he hadn't finished upsetting the loggers. What they did to Tom seemed unnecessary. There had to be more to it.

• • •

When he eventually dragged himself out of bed on Saturday, Jason woke his computer and loaded `Plan.doc`. There were the words that were haunting him: 'we must avoid close scrutiny'.

Scrutiny of what? What were the loggers trying to hide? They had the government's permission, and thinning was good for the forest, so why did they care if people knew what they were doing? Surely carting animal faeces from interstate just to stop a few protesters from watching them was overkill.

Jason read the whole document again, but it said exactly the same as it had every other time he'd read it. If only he could get access to the loggers' network! Some other file in `ProjectQuollifications` probably had the answer. But it would be stupid to try breaking into the loggers' depot again since they were bound to have tightened their security.

Jason started looking through the files on his laptop just in case Mr Wherrett had accidentally left something juicy there. While he was doing so, his phone signalled the arrival of a text. That wasn't so unusual, except this text came from 'Private number'. The message itself was strange, too:

Get a clue, tie a yellow ribbon

That didn't make any sense. Jason figured it was probably sent to him by mistake so he deleted it.

Still, something about it niggled at him. He mentioned it to his father at lunch time.

'Tie a yellow ribbon, eh?' said Mr Saunders. 'I remember that.'

Jason's mother burst into song: 'Tie a yellow ribbon round the ole oak tree….'

After begging her to stop, Jason thought about those lyrics. The mention of a tree made the message seem relevant, but didn't provide any information about what it meant. Some other words in the song might have yielded additional clues but Jason wasn't desperate enough to ask his mother to resume singing. The fate of the forest wasn't worth it.

'You know they tie ribbons around trees they're going to cut down?' said Mr Saunders.

Jason didn't, but he knew where he had to go after lunch.

●　　●　　●

Dad was right. Heaps of the gums in the forest were decked out with yellow plastic ribbons. The decorations glowed in the dappled sunlight. The scene would have been quite artistic if it hadn't meant death for so many trees. Jason reminded himself that thinning was good for the forest overall; he'd done the maths to prove it.

The text message must have been getting at this, but what was the actual clue? So what if there were ribbons? What about them?

Jason trudged along a walking track while he thought. A couple of times he caught himself scanning the ground for quoll poo, even though he'd been the one to reveal that there never was any. Well, not any that was locally produced.

His thinking was interrupted by the sound of distant footsteps. Thudding footsteps, running. Were they somehow related to the text that brought him here? Was it a trap?

He hunched down behind some bushes as the jogger puffed past. Judging from the sound effects, it was someone heavy and not very fit. Roscoe, maybe? That would make sense: Roscoe was the loggers' hit-man, and the loggers obviously had their suspicions about who was responsible for breaking into their depot and exposing their frame-up. They also knew Jason had the necessary computing skills.

Jason peeped through the foliage at the retreating runner. It wasn't Roscoe; it was David. Jason exhaled the breath he'd been holding. Some of his teasing about his friend's weight must have sunken in.

He jumped out from his hiding place and gave half a wave, but David's sweaty back didn't see it. He contemplated calling out but there was nothing to say, so he just watched the solid frame pound into the distance.

When David was out of sight, Jason resumed his mission. He trudged for over an hour, hoping to find the mysterious ribbon clue. But no clue appeared; all he could see were ribbons. Hundreds of ribbons, glowing yellower as the sun descended, with their tails waving in the breeze like they were taunting him. 'Hey, here we are, we know something you don't, and we're not telling.'

Jason stopped at a particularly large tree and tugged gently on its ribbon. It was only soft plastic and could easily be removed. Gillian could get the greenies to go through the forest and pull all the ribbons off. That would slow things down, at least.

But that wasn't Gillian's style, and the loggers would just put the ribbons back. The police would probably get involved, so the end result would be the same except for the greenies getting into trouble.

Jason took out his phone and snapped a couple of pictures of the tree and its ribbon. He then swivelled through 360 degrees and grabbed pictures of the trees around him. On the way home, he took more snaps every few minutes. Even though he couldn't work out what the ribbons meant right now, maybe he'd get an idea later on. If that happened, the pictures could come in handy.

He took so many photos that he filled up his phone's memory, so when he got home he moved them onto his laptop. They were easier to see on the laptop's bigger screen, anyway. He went through them and deleted a couple that were blurry. He set one as his desktop background, then sat staring at the yellow-flecked image.

But still he remained clueless.

Chapter 24

Logger Logic

Jason gave up trying to sleep at 4am. He realised he'd probably dozed for a few hours but it didn't feel like it. He'd had a brilliant idea not long after midnight and it just wouldn't wait until daylight to be tested.

As soon as his laptop started, Jason worked his way through the pictures he'd taken yesterday, counting the number of trees that had ribbons and the number that didn't. One of the numbers in his thinning spreadsheet was the percentage of trees to be cut down, and he'd originally found a value for that in the `Numbers.pdf` file he'd found on the loggers' network. After making a copy of the spreadsheet, he deleted that value and typed in an equation to work out the real value, using the numbers he'd counted on his pictures.

His hunch was right. The new spreadsheet showed the forest would deteriorate for decades with that amount of thinning. It was too much. The ribbons seemed to be suggesting that the loggers were going to cut down a lot more trees than `Numbers.pdf` said.

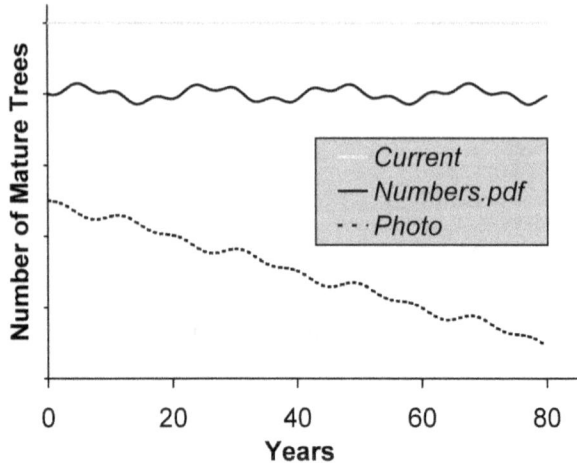

It was easy to be suspicious of the loggers, but maybe the `pdf` value meant something other than what he thought. Or maybe he'd simply made a mistake—yet again.

Jason pondered who he could get to check his work. His parents wouldn't help with anything that could result in him offending anyone else, especially the loggers. The only one from school who was still on speaking terms with him was Bull, and Bull wasn't exactly the intellectual type.

No, there was someone else from school: Chandra.

For the first time ever, Jason sensed a downside to school holidays. It would be two weeks until he saw the teacher again. Maybe the delay wouldn't matter, but Jason reminded himself that his tardiness in doing something about the quoll poo hadn't worked out well. He'd known Einstein was planning to trash the loggers' depot but he procrastinated, resulting in a fire that damaged the forest and several houses, including Emma's.

Of course, when he eventually *did* come out and accuse Tom, he was wrong. If he'd waited even longer, maybe he'd have worked out that it wasn't Tom at all, and Emma would still be talking to him.

•   •   •

There was something else that Jason had been putting off. After the log had been thrown through his window, Gillian had asked him to let her know if he ever found any evidence about who did it. Like everyone else, she was assuming it was one of the loggers. Since it wasn't actually a logger, Jason was tempted to not mention it to her; after all, she couldn't take the loggers to court for something one of her own people had done. But on the other hand, she still kept accusing the loggers and that wasn't fair to them.

Jason propped his bike against Gillian's cabin but didn't knock on the door straight away. Instead, he skulked down to the camping area of the caravan park. As he'd hoped, Einstein's ute was there and nobody was around. He quickly snapped a pic of the contents of the ute's tray, then retreated back to Gillian's place.

The lawyer swapped back and forth between the picture Jason had just taken and the one of the log on his breakfast table. After Jason showed her how, she zoomed in on both images and compared the saw marks. Jason didn't need to ask if she understood; her pursed lips showed she did.

'He said we needed revving up,' explained Jason.

'Unbelievable. I'd hoped Tom would be able to keep Einstein under control.'

Jason replied without thinking. 'He tried. He stopped Einstein from setting fire to the loggers' depot when we were there.'

Gillian sank down onto the sofa. After staring out the window for a while, she managed some words. 'I made everyone promise they wouldn't go near that place. They insisted they didn't do it. And I swore to everyone that it wasn't us.'

'I'm sorry,' said Jason. 'But we needed to—'

'I can't control this rabble,' said Gillian. She strode into the bedroom, pulled a suitcase down from the top of the wardrobe and tossed it onto the bed. 'They've never showed me any respect. I don't know why I've put up with this for so long.'

'Please don't—'

'Despite this criminal behaviour, we still haven't got a clue about how to stop the logging. I give up.'

Jason was itching to mention his latest spreadsheet but didn't dare. There was just too great a risk of being wrong. Gillian obviously wasn't in a listening mood anyway, and since Jason was as guilty as the others for the break-in, he wasn't in her good books either. His sheepish 'bye' went unacknowledged.

•　　•　　•

Gillian's imminent departure made Jason want to get his spreadsheet checked out as soon as possible. Fortunately Chandra hadn't gone away for the holidays, and he invited Jason to meet him at school on Monday morning.

Chandra compared Jason's new spreadsheet with its predecessor, then leaned back. 'I do not see any problem.'

'Yes you do,' said Jason. 'The spreadsheet that uses the info from my photos says there's too much thinning.'

Chandra's nose returned to the screen. Jason followed it to make sure the doctor was looking in the right place.

He was—but the spreadsheet clearly indicated that the level of thinning was fine. The forest went along very healthily.

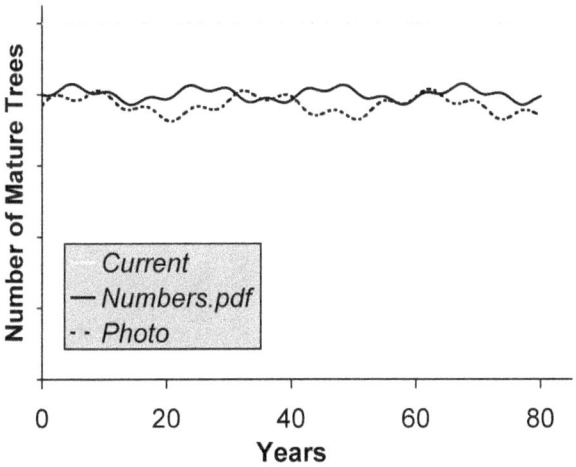

'That's funny,' said Jason. 'I'm sure it didn't say that yesterday.'

'Not to worry,' replied the teacher. 'You should not be doing this in your holidays. Go for a swim.'

Jason didn't. It was still too cold. But it was good weather for fixing spreadsheets. As soon as he got home, he opened up his laptop and stared at it. Had he copied the wrong file at some stage? Had he accidentally clicked undo?

The error was so obvious that Jason kicked himself for not spotting it when he was with Chandra. The spreadsheet's value for the percentage of trees that had ribbons on them was way too low; it was nearly as low as the value in Numbers.pdf. No wonder it said thinning was okay.[8]

Jason couldn't figure out how he could have stuffed up the value in the spreadsheet, but that didn't really matter. What mattered was that when the *actual* percentage of ribbons was put back in, the spreadsheet said there was too much thinning.

Jason was tempted to cycle back to school that afternoon but figured Chandra probably wouldn't want to see him again so soon. The teacher must have had some work to do at school or he wouldn't have been there. No matter; the spreadsheet would still show the same thing tomorrow morning.

•　　　•　　　•

'I am sorry,' said Chandra. 'I am not seeing it.'

Jason stared at the screen. 'But I checked it last night!' He took back his laptop and examined the spreadsheet cell that specified the percentage of trees with ribbons. Unlike yesterday morning, the value was right—but now the spreadsheet was saying that such a large amount of thinning was fine. The graph was pretty much the same as when he'd shown it to Chandra last time.

Jason flipped back to his original spreadsheet, the one that used the Numbers.pdf value for the amount of thinning.

'It is no wonder they both say thinning is good,' said the teacher. 'The amount of thinning is nearly the same in each of them.'[8]

Jason looked at the numbers. Chandra was right, but he shouldn't have been. 'I think this number is wrong,' said Jason, pointing at the cell that contained the amount of thinning from `Numbers.pdf`.

He started looking for `Numbers.pdf`. 'Why do spreadsheets keep changing things?' he asked as he searched. 'They're not very good if you can't trust them.'

Chandra leaned back and smirked. 'How often have I heard students blame computers for what their fingers do.'

'It was okay when it made changes to the quoll poo spreadsheet. They were good.'

'It really did that?'

'The network keeps changing too. I used to be able to get into a folder called `AFI` and now I can't. But that's probably because of the loggers.'

The doctor's smirk vanished. 'Let us try something.' He reached behind Jason's laptop and pulled out the modem.

'But now my internet won't work,' said Jason.

'Exactly.'

● ● ●

A knock at the front door pulled Jason up from the depths of concentration. The distraction was welcome because there was more going weird with his spreadsheet than a simple wrong number. Now, when he put the `Numbers.pdf` thinning value in, the silly computer said it was nowhere near enough, and much more thinning was required. It never said that before. Jason was getting the feeling that even if he did fix the spreadsheet, it would just break again of its own accord.[8]

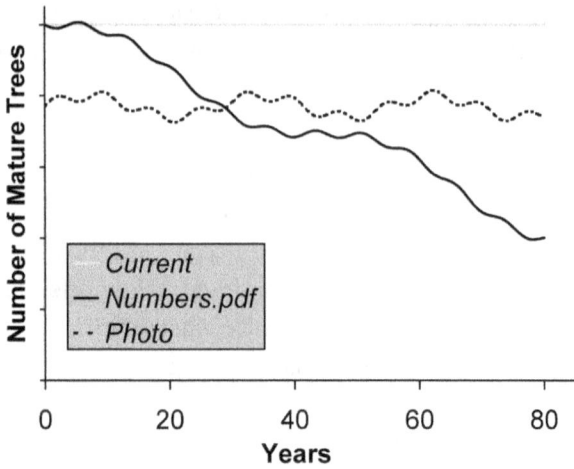

Mrs Saunders was in the back yard so Jason opened the door, then took a step back.

'May we come in?' asked Mr Wherrett, although he and Roscoe didn't wait for an answer before entering. 'I thought I should clear the air with you. I hope you know you don't need to avoid us because of the break-in,' he said, while looking around the lounge room. Roscoe's eyes were roving too.

Jason nodded slowly, while trying to work out what the visitors were looking for.

'The greenies obviously did it,' continued Mr Wherrett, 'but we know you're not one of them any more.'

Roscoe gave a nod in the direction of the kitchen.

'Ah, your computer,' said Mr Wherrett, striding to the kitchen table where Jason had the machine set up since there wasn't any clear space in his bedroom. The logger walked around the laptop, inspecting it from all angles. 'Is it running okay?' he asked.

Jason realised that `Numbers.pdf` was on the screen, so he closed the file. 'It's running fine.'

'Here's the problem,' said Mr Wherrett, spotting the modem inside the laptop's bag. He grabbed it and inserted it into one of the computer's USB ports.

'I was just trying something,' explained Jason.

'You can't. You have to have a permanent connection. It was in the agreement you signed.'

'Get a clue,' added Roscoe in his usual gruff tone.

Jason sat down. Something was going on with the modem. Chandra was obviously onto it, but what was it?

'I know,' said Jason slowly. 'If I fix the spreadsheet, it'll just change again, won't it? You can change it using your network, can't you?'[9]

Mr Wherrett laughed and sat down beside Jason. 'I was just messing with you. I wondered how long you'd take to work it out.' He laughed again, but it seemed forced.

'No,' said Jason. 'I counted the ribbons. I think you're going to cut down more trees than you're allowed to.' He rotated his legs out from under the table so he could make a quick getaway if Roscoe made a move for him, but the big logger remained standing behind his boss, listening intently.

Mr Wherrett shook his head. 'One of the numbers in your spreadsheet is wrong. The EIA figure is higher than what you keep putting in there.'

Jason thought about that. What did the logger mean by 'EIA figure'? That must be the thinning value in `Numbers.pdf`. So `Numbers.pdf` must be the EIA.

'No, I checked,' said Jason. 'I kept a copy of your EIA thing.'

'I don't think so. I scanned your computer for it. You're just going by memory since you can't access our network any more.'

'My copy isn't called E I A.'

'Oh.' Mr Wherrett clenched his jaw. 'I wonder what else you've got on that computer....'

Ribbon photos, thought Jason. He pulled the computer towards himself just in case the logger was thinking about trying to take it back.

'Everyone wants wood and paper,' said Mr Wherrett, looking out a window to where Jason's mother was hammering a stake into the garden. 'If we don't produce it in Australia, someone else will have to produce more. Like in Indonesia and the Amazon. Compared to what's happening in those places, we're only one small company so it won't make much difference what we do.'

'I know where you got that from,' said Jason, screwing up his face. 'Mr Lindsay.'

'Did he say that? No, I heard it from Jason Saunders.'

'When did I?' asked Jason indignantly, although he knew it was possible.

'When you vandalised our sign. I'll bet you use the same excuse for stealing software and wasting petrol—not to mention breaking into our depot.'

Jason's chest tightened. He wanted to ask how Mr Wherrett found out about that but couldn't work out how to do so without basically admitting his guilt.

'So you, me and the Prime Minister basically agree,' continued the logger. 'If something was going to happen anyway, it doesn't matter who does it. Especially if you're only a small player.'

For the sake of the forest, Jason didn't want to agree but there was no faulting Mr Wherrett's logic. 'I guess….'

'I knew you'd understand. The problem is, most people aren't as smart as you. They mightn't get it. That's why we need to be careful who finds out.'

'You want me to keep your secret even though you used me to get Tom in trouble?' Jason tried not to make eye contact with Roscoe, even though the hulk was being surprisingly well behaved.

Mr Wherrett bit his lower lip. 'I'm sorry about that. But take it as a compliment: I picked you because nobody else in this town would have been smart enough to put the clues together.'

There was a bang from the back yard as Mrs Saunders closed the shed door.

'If I told my parents you'd been spying on me,' said Jason, 'you'd be in deep poo.'

'But you can't, can you? Because you've been spying on me too, including breaking into my office.'

'But if I hadn't done it, then….' Jason stopped himself from telling the logger about Einstein's plans.

'Would your parents let you off because something was going to happen anyway? See what I mean about how other people don't get it?'

Once again, Jason didn't want to agree but the argument seemed watertight. He stared fiercely at his laptop.

'I know you're not a bad kid,' continued Mr Wherrett. 'You've never lied, and whenever you've done things other people didn't approve of, you thought it was okay because those things were going to happen anyway. Just like our logging. So can I trust you not to tell anyone?'

Jason fiddled with the salt and pepper shakers.

'So can I trust you?' repeated Mr Wherrett.

Jason's mother walked in. 'Of course you can trust him,' she said. 'Can't he, Jason?'

'I guess,' said Jason, still clanking the shakers.

Mrs Saunders didn't look satisfied with that. 'What do you mean, "you guess"?'

'Okay, yes, you can trust me. Totally.'

Jason's mother escorted the visitors to the front door while Jason stayed sitting at his computer. So Mr Wherrett was monitoring his files, was he? Presumably he hadn't discovered the ribbon photos, but just to be safe, Jason moved them out of My Documents and into an obscure folder under Windows.

Mrs Saunders eventually finished apologising to Mr Wherrett for Jason's rudeness and closed the front door. The vigour of her footsteps as she returned to the kitchen warned Jason to prepare for an onslaught.

'I don't know what's got into you, Jason. You're rude to the loggers, you've upset the protesters, you hang around with thugs, you deface other people's property, and you're in trouble at school.'

There was nothing deniable in that list, so Jason just shrugged his shoulders.

That response didn't appease his mother too much. 'All this started when you got involved with this forest thing. From now on, I don't want you to have anything to do with it.'

'But....' But there wasn't a 'but', really. The greenies had given up, the loggers were going to trash the forest, and Jason's mother had made him promise not to tell Mr Wherrett's dirty little secret even though she had no idea what was going on. He had no reason to see the loggers or the greenies again anyway. 'Fine. But you can't blame me for any of it.'

'Oh really?'

'I'm only one small person. It doesn't make any difference what I do. Mr Lindsay taught me that.'

'So your bad behaviour is the Prime Minister's fault, is it?' said Jason's mother. 'Ooo-kay, I know how to deal with this.'

Jason didn't like the vibe of that. It sounded like a decision had been made. 'How?' he asked.

'You'll see.'

Chapter 25

Killing Two Birds with One Plan

How *dare* she? What did she think the PM was going to achieve? Was the politician simply going to order Jason to be a good boy, thus curing all his problems?

Jason reluctantly followed his mother into the lounge room, where Mr Lindsay was waiting with Jason's father. After the obligatory handshake, they all sat down.

'Did you really come all the way here just to see me?' asked Jason. 'Don't you have to run the country?'

The PM laughed. 'You're not the only one who's entitled to the occasional holiday. Don't forget that my beach house is just up the coast a bit.'

'—where you get all those rips.'

'Jason!' snapped Mrs Saunders.

'Yes, there,' said Mr Lindsay. 'Speaking of rips, I understand you're having a few problems of your own.'

'No.'

'Yes.' Jason's mother obviously wasn't going to let him get out of this easily. She glared at him, and he glared back.

'Would it be okay if I talked to my lifesaver alone?' asked the PM. 'Maybe you could show me the forest, Jason.'

Mrs Saunders looked disappointed, but agreed to the request.

'Shall we take your car or mine?' Mr Lindsay asked Jason as they left the house.

'Yours would probably be quicker.'

Jason navigated them to the picnic area, where the quoll search had left from. As they got out of the PM's Camry, a black Commodore pulled up beside them and two black-suited security guards emerged.

The group walked into the forest. Even though it was Sunday afternoon and a nice spring day, there was nobody else about. The guards stayed about ten metres behind Jason and Mr Lindsay, which made Jason feel like looking over his shoulder all the time.

'That's a lot of ribbons,' remarked the PM.

Jason grunted.

Mr Lindsay tried to make small talk about school, cars, and even the weather, but Jason didn't want to play. He was still annoyed about his mother's meddling and her stupid assumption that the PM could fix everything when he was actually part of the problem.

After a while, the PM gave up trying to be chummy. 'Your mother's told me what's been happening with you this year. Here's my theory. You've got yourself tangled up in something and you're doing the wrong thing. But you know what the right thing is, and the fact that you're not doing it is screwing you up.'

Jason was impressed at how much sense that made, considering Mr Lindsay had no idea what was really going on. But Jason wasn't really doing anything wrong at the moment: he was just keeping Mr Wherrett's secret like he promised. Plus, Mr Wherrett had made it hard to work out what the 'right thing' actually was—using the PM's own logic.

'There's stuff happening here you don't know about,' said Jason.

'Tell me.'

'I can't. Anyway, you wouldn't get it, because they're only doing the same as you.'

Mr Lindsay gave an exasperated grimace. 'Your mother said I had something to do with it, but I can't deal with it unless you tell me what's going on.'

But Jason couldn't. He'd said he wouldn't and he'd have been wasting his breath on the PM anyway.

They trudged on in silence. At one point, Mr Lindsay halted and pointed with one of his dress shoes at a deposit on the ground. 'Quoll?' he asked. Jason assured him it was only kangaroo.

The track eventually returned them to the picnic area. 'Well,' said Mr Lindsay as they got into his car, 'for all that walking, we didn't get very far, did we? I still don't know how I can help you.'

'I don't think you want to get involved,' replied Jason.

'I really do care about how you're going. Because you saved my life, I feel like we're somehow bound together.'

'The TV thinks so, too.'

'Yes,' said the PM, frowning. 'You know I can't afford to be linked to the bunfight over the forest here. But that's another matter entirely.'

•   •   •

After clashing with greenies, loggers, parents, and even the Prime Minister, Jason welcomed the return of the drudgery of school. Of course, there were still clashes to avoid since Emma and David had dumped him, and it would be best to avoid Bull until the issue with his mother was sorted out.

At least one set of clashes Jason had avoided for the last few months was debating, since he'd quit the club. In preparation for an inter-school competition, there was a practice session for the debating team in the school hall just before lunchtime. Even though the whole school was supposed to watch, Jason had no intention of doing so— until he was spotted by Ms Gow as he was heading in the opposite direction to everyone else.

Jason found a clearing in the centre of the hall that was nicely equidistant from the patrolling teachers. The only downside of the location was that it was just in front of David, who nodded vaguely as Jason settled in.

Jason nodded back. 'Saw you running in the forest the other week. Losing weight?'

'Supposed to be, but aren't. The coach says I'm getting fitter and stronger, but.'

'I guess that's good.'

'I guess.'

The debate was annoying. The debaters kept making fundamental errors, like saying 'um' and reading from their notes. Jason couldn't help but criticise their mistakes out loud. After a few such comments, David poked him in the back and told him to 'shhh'.

That was easier said than done. Jason tried to distract himself by thinking about how to get out of his promise not to tell anyone about the loggers, and how to make Mr Lindsay understand that it was his fault, sort of. Jason had finally gotten his wish: he'd never really wanted to be involved, and now he was out of the game. But that didn't stop him caring about the result.

'You can't say that,' he exclaimed, as a statement by one of debaters broke through his attempt to block them out. 'That's an "appeal to the masses".'

David prodded him in the back again. 'You wimped out the debating club, remember? Quit trying to play from the sideline.'

Jason realised David was right. Not just about debating, but about the whole logger-PM mess. But how could he get back in the game after his mother had thrown him out of the comp? Plus, if he wanted the loggers to do the right thing, he should be prepared do the right thing too, and that meant keeping his word about not telling anyone.

●   ●   ●

'I'm not surprised it doesn't work in the photocopier,' said the lady in the Student Services office as she inspected Jason's scratched-up student card. 'What have you been doing with it?'

'Just using it,' replied Jason. That was totally true. If the lady had wanted to know whether he'd been using it to break into the loggers' depot, she should have asked.

'You know there's a five dollar fee to replace a lost card?' she asked.

'But it isn't lost. It's in your hand.'

The lady looked unimpressed but handed over a new card. For free.

●   ●   ●

Jason had made sure he didn't have Ms Gow for English this term. Hopefully his new teacher, Ms Gellibrand, knew nothing of his previous issues with Ms Gow and her family.

Unfortunately, changing English teachers meant having to take a unit that couldn't possibly be relevant to anything: *Analysis of the Novel*. Ms Gellibrand had already told the class what they had to read and was now crapping on about what writing features to look for.

'When something's important, good authors use the principle *show, don't tell*,' she said. 'For example, instead of "John was angry", they'd write "John punched the wall". This gives readers a mental picture like they'd see in real life, and lets them work out for themselves what it means.'

'Show, don't tell,' murmured Jason. His concentration switched off English and reverted to logging. A plan started to form. It could be put into action without confronting Mr Wherrett, but that would be messy because the media would get involved. It would be better if the logger just decided to do the right thing of his own accord—or at least in response to a little nudge. And that meant visiting him to administer the nudge.

There was even a chance the plan might get through to Mr Lindsay and make him re-adopt the emission control targets. If Jason considered that to be part of the plan, then he wouldn't be visiting Mr Wherrett about the forest, as he'd promised his mother he wouldn't. Instead, he'd be visiting Mr Wherrett about global warming, and Mrs Saunders never said he couldn't do that. Getting the emission controls back would definitely be a great bonus.

But the most amazing thing about the plan was that it had come out of an English class.

Chapter 26

Showdown

Jason sat on the ground with his back against the loggers' sign. David hadn't showed up. That was disappointing, but not totally surprising.

Maybe he didn't get the text. Jason checked his phone to make sure it had gone okay.

Message sent 1:53pm today: 'Ive quit trying to play from sideline. Cud use ur help. Meet me @ loggers sign after school?'

That looked fine, but school had finished almost an hour ago. If David was going to come, he'd have made it by now.

Proceeding alone was risky. Having a second pair of eyes and ears could have been helpful if something unexpected happened. A parent wasn't an option because they'd think the 'show, don't tell' plan was only about logging, so they'd close the loophole Jason was using to justify visiting Mr Wherrett. Emma wasn't an option because she was avoiding Jason, and Bull wasn't an option because Jason was avoiding him.

Jason figured there was no point putting the plan on hold while waiting for a new ally to come into his life. The loggers would be finished marking trees any day now, and then the felling would start. Plus, if this mess didn't get sorted out soon, there'd be no concentrating at school for yet another term, and that wouldn't go down well at home. Given a choice between one last discussion with Mr Wherrett versus another poor report card, his parents would be much more likely to forgive the former.

Jason got up, slung the strap of his laptop bag over his shoulder, and marched towards the loggers' depot. Mr Wherrett should be the only one there, since the actual loggers would be out in the forest at this time.

As he ascended the steps to the demountable's door, Jason looked over his shoulder to see if David was behind him. He wasn't. Jason bit his lower lip, knocked twice, then pushed the door open.

'I didn't expect to see you again,' said Mr Wherrett, looking up from his paperwork.

Jason swallowed. 'Please don't cut down more trees than you're supposed to. You should do the right thing for the forest. And to make Mr Lindsay understand.'

The logger looked baffled for a moment, then recovered. 'And if I don't "do the right thing", you'll tell on me? But shouldn't you do the right thing too? That means keeping your word.'

'I promised not to tell, and I won't.'

'Then, what?' Mr Wherrett slumped back in his chair and motioned for Jason to sit opposite him.

Jason explained how cutting down extra trees only made sense because of what Mr Lindsay had said when he wimped out of the emission controls. So, if Mr Lindsay changed his mind, then the extra logging would have to stop.

'But you can't get Mr Lindsay to change his mind, can you?'

'No, but maybe you can.'

The logger went back to looking confused. 'I can't see how, and I'm not sure I want to.'

Jason wasn't really surprised. It did sound pretty confusing, like a circular reference his spreadsheet used to complain about. He attempted to explain in different ways, but it seemed like Mr Wherrett had no intention of even trying to understand.

'As far as I'm concerned,' said the logger, 'you still have to keep your secret.'

'I've been thinking about that. Like you said, everybody's doing it. Doing stuff or taking stuff because it doesn't make much difference.'

'So?'

'So you don't need to keep what you're doing a secret. Everyone will understand because it's the same as what they do.'

Mr Wherrett raised his eyebrows and nodded. 'That actually makes sense. You might be right. But I don't intend to find out.'

Jason realised there was no way he was going to win with words, so he opened up his laptop.

The logger slumped back in his chair again and exhaled. 'I can see we're not going to resolve this quickly. Let me make sure we don't get any interruptions.' He pulled out his mobile phone and started fiddling with it. Jason was surprised how long it took him to work out how to mute it, considering how good he was at hacking into other people's computers.

Jason called up a gallery of the pictures he'd taken in the forest. As he was doing so, he heard a dull clunk behind him. He looked around but couldn't see anything; hopefully it was just the loggers coming back from the forest.

'Very pretty,' said Mr Wherrett, after Jason had turned the laptop to face him. 'Oh wait, I get it. You're threatening to post your pictures on the internet. But you can't, because you said you wouldn't.'

'I said I wouldn't *tell*,' said Jason. 'But this would be *showing*, so it would be okay.'

'I disagree.' Mr Wherrett went to pull the laptop towards himself but Jason grabbed it back.

'There's no point taking my computer. Everything's backed up on the internet.'

'I don't think so. I' know exactly what's in your My Documents folder.'

'I know you do.' That's why I moved them out of there.'

'Then they won't be backed up, will they?'

Oops! The logger was almost certainly right. That changed things. Jason closed the image gallery and started the email program.

'So you're storing files where you think I can't find them, are you?' said Mr Wherrett. 'There's more than one way for me to see what's on there.' He leaned forward and reached for the laptop but Jason pulled it away from him.

The logger scowled, then got up and started to creep around the side of his desk.

Jason sprang to his feet. He balanced the laptop on his left arm while the fingers of his right hand flashed over the keyboard.

'Put the computer down,' said Mr Wherrett, edging closer.

All of a sudden, the super-laptop seemed agonisingly slow. 'It's my computer. If you take it, or break it, you'll get into trouble.' Jason's digits continued to dance as he backed away from the logger. On reaching the door, he stopped typing for long enough to confirm his suspicion that it had been locked from the outside.

'Thank you, Roscoe,' said Mr Wherrett, tapping his phone.

The logger kept coming and Jason kept retreating without shifting his focus from the email he was composing. Out of the corner of his eye he saw a hand swipe at the modem, which was sticking out from one side of the laptop. 'You can't do that,' he said, swivelling sideways. 'You said the modem has to stay inserted.'

'Smart-arse.' Mr Wherrett made another lame grab at the computer but Jason jumped out of the way, accidentally knocking over a coat rack in the process. The laptop nearly escaped in the process. Leaping backwards in a cramped office with a computer balanced on one arm was not something you could get away with too many times.

Jason finished attaching the pictures to the email then hit Send, but the stupid email program wouldn't send it without a subject. Showdown, thought Jason, and started typing as quickly as his circumstances allowed.

Just as he was about to retry `Send`, Jason's adversary lunged again. Once more, Jason leapt without looking. Unfortunately he'd forgotten about the coffee table, and one of his feet hooked the table as his body sailed over it. In slow-motion, he saw the laptop lift off from his arm and embark on an independent trajectory across the room, closely followed by an airborne Mr Wherrett.

Jason was the first to hit the floor. It hurt. A lot. His arms had been busy with the computer and his legs had been trapped behind him by the coffee table, so there was nothing to break his fall but the side of his face. He lay stunned, his vision blurred—but not so blurred he couldn't see Mr Wherrett crash into the base of a tall bookcase, which toppled forward and pinned him down.

Jason tried to get up, but his body wouldn't obey. He ordered it and he begged it, but nothing happened.

Fortunately the logger wasn't doing any better. He tried to raise himself like he was doing a push-up but the bookcase was too heavy. His grunts were interspersed with a mixture of threats and swearing.

The remains of the laptop were lying nearby. The screen was dangling loose and was only connected to the rest of it by a few wires. A crack ran the length of the chassis. Ironically, the modem was still plugged in, though.

Jason tried to recall whether he'd managed to press `Send` while in mid-air. If so, would the computer have had enough time to transmit the email while it was en route to the floor? If it never got to utter its potentially famous last words, it will have died for nothing.

Come on, body. Let's get out of here. Jason tried to marshal his limbs but his head hurt too much. He wanted to be running down the road well before Mr Wherrett managed to extricate himself, but that didn't look like it was going to happen since the logger was already pulling his body out from under the furniture.

After a brief clatter, the door burst open and David barged in. He quickly surveyed the trashed office, then hustled over to Mr Wherrett's bookcase and dropped his bulky frame onto it.

'Oooph,' went the body below as the air was squeezed from its lungs. The logger thrashed his limbs around like an inverted turtle trying to turn over, but he didn't stand a chance with David on board.

'Can you get up?' asked David.

'No, you fat moron,' wheezed Mr Wherrett. 'You're sitting on me.'

'Hey, a talking bookcase. I didn't mean you. You smashed my friend's computer, so you can stay there.'

'I didn't break it. He did it himself. I made sure of that.'

It was then that Jason noticed Roscoe. He tried to warn David but could only manage to point and make a gurgling sound.

'He's cool,' said David. 'He unlocked the door when I told him you were here.'

'Get this slob off me,' demanded Mr Wherrett.

Roscoe ignored the instruction and looked around, while his boss's language became more explicit. 'You okay?' he asked Jason, tapping him on the side with a boot.

Jason tried to get up and failed, so the bald logger lifted him to his feet and steadied him while he relearnt how to balance upright. After a while, the room stopped swaying and stayed in focus.

'Take my bike,' said David.

'What about you?'

'I'll run. I need to lose weight.'

'Yes, you do.' Jason took another look at his friend pinning down Mr Wherrett. 'No, you don't. Thanks.'

Roscoe tipped his head in the direction of the door. 'Scram. Get a clue.'

Chapter 27

Getting the Message

The debating club meeting was running behind schedule. After he'd finished practicing his speech, Jason had to leave or he would have been late for work. He jumped on his bike and headed into town.

A couple of days had passed since Operation Showdown. The confrontation with Mr Wherrett hadn't gone as smoothly as Jason had hoped. It had taken Jason a while to work out what the logger had meant about breaking the computer. He'd never intended to break it himself; he was just trying to get Jason to do it so he couldn't be blamed. Very clever.

Jason had played straight into Mr Wherrett's hands in that regard, but it was still possible that the logger might play into Jason's hands regarding the whole point of Operation Showdown. The plan now depended entirely on other people, starting with Gillian. As he'd done about every fifteen minutes for the last two days, Jason checked his phone for any messages from the lawyer. As usual, there weren't any.

Nobody had been able to contact Gillian since she'd left Sapphire Bay. Tom had said she was 'going bush' for a while before returning to Sydney, so she probably didn't have mobile phone coverage. Until she returned to civilisation, there was no way to know whether she'd received the Showdown email or not.

Even though there was no sign of life from Gillian, the loggers had been busy. They'd taken down at least half the ribbons from the forest, as Jason suspected they would. His photos were now the only evidence of what Mr Wherrett had been planning. Obviously the photos on his laptop were history, and he'd checked his phone in the hope that he hadn't deleted the originals, but he had. The only set in existence was waiting for Gillian on some email server somewhere—assuming the Showdown email had actually been sent before the laptop died.

Jason still hadn't told his parents about the demise of his laptop. Even if they won lotto, they probably wouldn't fork out to replace it since he'd broken it while clashing with Mr Wherrett. If Gillian came through and exposed the loggers they might take a more lenient view, but that was a big if.

Jason figured the surest way to get a new computer was to save up for one himself. He locked his bike outside McDonald's and went in. Fortunately, he hadn't burnt his bridges too badly when he quit so the manager was willing to take him on again.

As they'd arranged, David lobbed in just after the start of Jason's shift. Jason took his friend's order at his table, then went out the back to prepare the meal personally. He dropped an extra meat patty into each burger, and two extra slices of cheese. Since David had saved his bacon, Jason threw some of that in too.

•   •   •

'Come on Mum, it's starting.'

Mrs Saunders joined Jason and his father in front of the TV. 'You normally couldn't care less about the news,' she said suspiciously.

'Today, I could.'

Friday's local news didn't let Jason down:

Australian Forestry Industries' contract for logging in Sapphire State Forest has been suspended pending a police investigation. Photographic evidence circulating on the internet suggests that the company intended to breach the terms of its contact by substantially exceeding the felling quota specified in the Environmental Impact Assessment.

One of Jason's photos was showing in the background behind the newsreader.

'The bastards!' exclaimed Jason's father.

Mrs Saunders looked at Jason. 'You knew this would be on, didn't you?'

Jason patted his mobile phone. Gillian had texted him that morning. The lawyer had played her part in the plan, and soon it would be Mr Wherrett's turn. The final victory, trapping Mr Lindsay, depended on how well the logger played his part—even though he didn't know he was playing a part. Jason had taught him his lines and encouraged him to deliver them, but Mr Wherrett might still get stage fright. Hopefully, when the spotlight was on him and he didn't have any choice, he'd rise to the occasion.

The TV continued:

A spokesman for Australian Forestry Industries, Florian Wherrett, didn't attempt to deny the allegations. 'I really think this issue is being blown out of all proportion. What we're doing won't make much difference overall. Everyone behaves like this, so what's the problem?'

'Beautiful,' said Jason quietly. 'Perfect.'

Chapter 28

On Heat

Jason's parents had been understandably conflicted about their son's role in exposing the loggers. Obviously they were nauseatingly proud of his triumph, but they were annoyed he hadn't left the issue alone after he'd been told to. 'You're lucky you didn't get hurt,' said Mrs Saunders, which provided the best opportunity Jason figured he was going to get to announce that his laptop did indeed get hurt.

After lunch on Monday, Jason had a session with Chandra. He wasn't looking forward to it because he'd have to tell the teacher he hadn't done the exercises he'd been set because he'd accidentally thrown his laptop across somebody's office. That sounded about as credible as 'the dog ate my homework'.

'Have you still got the laptop?' asked Chandra.

'It was trashed.'

'Laptop disk drives are rugged. It might be possible to get your files off it.'

Jason's eyes lit up. Multiple school assignments had been on there, and redoing them all from the start was going to be a pain.

After school, Jason explained the situation to his father. Mr Saunders revealed he was going to see Mr Newell that evening, to try to talk him out of taking any legal action against Jason for breaking in and stealing information. Conveniently, the boss of the logging company was in Sapphire Bay to help with the investigation into Mr Wherrett's activities. If the meeting went well, it would be a good opportunity to ask about the remains of the laptop.

Jason and his father bumped down the road to the loggers' depot in the 4WD they'd borrowed from Mr McKenzie. Jason couldn't help but remark on how much smoother the trip would have been in his Predator, even though he knew what his father's response would be: 'You shouldn't have dinged it up, then.' No surprises there.

There were several unfamiliar vehicles in the loggers' compound. Obviously things were pretty busy for the loggers at the moment.

Mr Saunders knocked on the door of the demountable. Jason was hugely relieved when the voice that responded wasn't Mr Wherrett's. His old adversary wasn't there. Instead, Mr Newell was sitting at Mr Wherrett's desk, and Gillian was sitting opposite him.

'You're busy,' said Jason's father. 'We'll come back later.'

'No, your timing is perfect,' replied Mr Newell. 'We were just talking about you.' He dragged two more chairs over to the desk.

Mr Saunders got straight to the point. 'Jason did some things he shouldn't have done. He's only young, so I'm hoping you'll cut him a break. I can offer you a good deal on some fish….'

The boss logger laughed. 'I've heard the fish and chips are good here, but that won't be necessary.'

'Before you arrived this evening,' said Gillian, 'I was just telling Adam that it was Jason who stopped the second attempt to burn this place down.'

Jason looked surprised. 'Oh yeah, I guess I did.'

'I'm disgusted at what Florian tried to do,' said Mr Newell, pointing to a tangle of dirty yellow ribbons piled up in a corner of the office. 'I should have been onto him. Jason was really just doing my job for me.'

Jason looked around the office. The bookshelf that had pinned Mr Wherrett down had been restored to the vertical, although it had a chunk missing from one corner. There was no sign of the laptop.

Mr Newell detected Jason's scan and gave him a quizzical look.

'I was wondering what happened to my computer,' said Jason.

'There wasn't any hope for it, I'm afraid,' replied Mr Newell. 'When I got here, Florian was trying its disk drive in his own computer but it wouldn't work.'

'Oh. Shame.'

Gillian stared fixedly at the logger.

'My company will replace your laptop, of course,' added Mr Newell hurriedly. 'After all, it's our fault that you broke it.'

'Wow, thanks!' said Jason. 'But don't worry about the modem. I'll get my own.'

•　　　•　　　•

Jason's mobile phone rang. Loudly.

'You're supposed to have it on silent in the library,' said David as Jason scrambled to find the device. Several people looked over to see who was responsible for the interruption—including Emma, who was sitting a few desks over. Jason fancied she cracked half a smile, but maybe that was just wishful thinking.

The phone had gravitated to the bottom of Jason's bag. He was surprised it was still ringing when he finally managed to answer it. 'Mr Saunders, please hold for the Prime Minister.'

This might be it, thought Jason. It was almost a week since Mr Wherrett had been on TV, when he started off the bonus level in Jason's game-plan without realising it.

Jason put a finger over the phone's microphone. 'You'll have to excuse me,' he told David. 'The Prime Minister needs my help again.'

David screwed up a piece of graph paper and threw it at Jason.

'I saw your Mr Wherrett on TV a couple of days ago,' said Mr Lindsay.

Jason nodded, then said 'good' when he realised the PM couldn't see him.

'My first reaction was that they should lock that guy up. But don't tell anyone I said that.'

'I won't,' promised Jason. 'What was your second reaction?'

'I've suggested to my colleagues that we need to have another think about our position on the Rotterdam emission control targets. But don't tell anyone I said that, either.'

'So you got it.'

'I didn't want to, but yes, I got it. What that logger said was too close for comfort. And it's only a matter of time before the media gets it too. You didn't leave me anywhere to go, did you?'

'That was the plan,' said Jason.

'All I can say is "well played". I also understand why you were behaving the way you were, although I can't condone illegal acts.'

Jason nodded again. 'I couldn't work out how to get emission controls back, but all I had to do was act feral. Next time I want something, I'll know what to do.'

'Next time, you'll be old enough to go to jail.'

• • •

Jason woke on Saturday to the realisation he'd have to survive another weekend without a computer. Mr Newell had texted during the week to say he hadn't forgotten his promise to replace the laptop, so Jason checked to see if there was an update on the matter. There wasn't, but while looking, he noticed the old text from Greasy with the license key for *Grand Theft Auto*. It wouldn't feel right to install GTA illegally again, now that the PM had rolled over and admitted you shouldn't be greedy just because everyone else is. Jason deleted the message.

One activity that didn't require a computer was to check the forest to see if the loggers had removed any more ribbons. After a 10am breakfast, Jason cycled to the picnic area. There were definitely less ribbons visible from there, but perhaps Mr Wherrett had just removed some of them from easily-accessible areas to mislead the police investigators.

Figuring there may be more ribbons further into the forest, Jason struck out along the track that headed towards Mount Gore. It wasn't long before he reached the area where the fire had burnt through. There were already signs of new growth, although the outskirts of the town could still be seen through the charred trees. The yellow tarpaulin on the roof of Emma's house, glowing in the morning sun, was hard to miss.

Jason spotted a small group of loggers walking through the forest in the distance. It hadn't occurred to him they'd be working on a Saturday. Mr Newell obviously wasn't wasting any time cleaning up his company's act.

Jason didn't fancy meeting the workers. Most of them were about as sophisticated as Einstein and wouldn't have appreciated his interference with their business. He contemplated skulking over to Emma's house, but since the loggers weren't heading in his direction, he just crouched out of sight.

The gang made slow progress, removing every ribbon in its path. Jason sat down with his back to a relatively unburnt eucalypt and monitored the situation through the bushes.

'Boo.'

Even though the voice behind him was obviously Emma's, Jason jolted. 'Oh, hi.'

'Hiding?' Emma asked, nodding towards the loggers.

'Watching.'

'Riiight.' Emma sat down against a tree a couple of metres away. 'Dad says I was silly for blaming you when he didn't. Especially considering *he* was the one you accused.'

That made Jason happier than he could find words to express, so he just smiled. The pair sat in silence and watched the ribbons coming down. Occasionally the sound of raucous laughter reached them.

'Why are they taking *all* the ribbons?' asked Emma. 'Don't they still have to do the thinning?'

'Mr Newell said it's up to the government. And it might be some other company next time.'

'Good. Serves them right.'

Jason lobbed a pebble at the remains of a fallen tree about twenty metres away.

'Missed,' said Emma.

'Best two out of three.' A second pebble hit the decaying wood with a dull tap.

So did the third, causing a small animal to emerge from behind the log. Jason thought he saw white spots on its back, but it was hard to be sure in the dappled light. The animal stared at the onlookers for a few seconds, then scurried off.

'Was that what I think it was?' asked Emma under her breath.

'Dunno. I'm mainly familiar with their poo.'

The pair kept their eyes trained on the direction in which the animal had departed. Occasional rustling sounds indicated its route.

'Let's follow it,' said Emma. 'Maybe it'll leave some droppings. I could take some home to Dad.'

They set off as quietly as they could. They spotted their quarry again after only a few paces, although it was already a long way ahead of them. It obviously heard them coming, and turned to face them for just long enough to leave a deposit on the forest floor.

Emma bounded after the animal as it disappeared between the trees, but Jason locked his eyes on the spot where it had just been and walked towards it. By the time Emma returned from her unsuccessful chase, Jason was on all fours inspecting a small pile on the ground.

'Well?' asked Emma, between pants.

'Fox. Which is probably just as well.'

'Why?'

'Your father mightn't react well if he sees any more animal droppings.'

Emma paused. 'You're right. This time for sure.'

A Note from the Author

Thank you for reading my book. If you enjoyed it, please take a moment to leave a review at your favourite retailer.

Peter McLennan

About the Author

Peter McLennan served for twenty-eight years in the Royal Australian Air Force, where he focused on strategic planning. He has tertiary qualifications in engineering, information science and government, and a PhD in planning for uncertainty. He has had several non-fiction monographs and papers published.

Peter now writes fiction from his home in Canberra. His hobbies include playing computer games badly and developing software badly.

Other Titles by Peter McLennan

Who Will Save the Planet?
(available from Amazon.com and other retail outlets)

Connect with Peter McLennan

Home page:
http://writer.catplace.net

goodreads:
http://www.goodreads.com/author/show/
5829977.Peter_McLennan

Twitter:
http://www.twitter.com/petermcl

Facebook:
http://www.facebook.com/
profile.php?id=100001079509514

Notes

Note 1 (page 112): Thinning

Ecological thinning is a real thing, although there is disagreement about how beneficial it is. Thinning trials are being conducted in parts of Australia. You can read more about it on *Wikipedia* (http://en.wikipedia.org/wiki/Ecological_Thinning).

Note 2 (page 113): Iteration

In mathematics and computing, the process of calculating things by going around in circles like this is called *iteration*. For an example of a simple equation that seems to depend on itself, assume that a field has 100 rabbits in it, and the population doubles every year. This can be written:

$R_{y+1} = R_y \times 2$

where R_y is the number of rabbits at the start of year y, and R_{y+1} is the number of rabbits at the start of year y+1.

Here's an example of how to use this equation:

$R_0 = 100$
$R_1 = R_0 \times 2 = 100 \times 2 = 200$
$R_2 = R_1 \times 2 = 200 \times 2 = 400$
$R_3 = R_2 \times 2 = 400 \times 2 = 800$

and so on. You can see how the answer from the equation in one year gets fed back into the equation for the next year, and this cycle repeats.

Obviously it would take quite a while to use this method to work out how many rabbits there'd be after twenty years. It would take even longer if the equation was more complicated. And if you made a mistake early on, all the results for subsequent years would be wrong, so you'd have to repeat virtually the whole process to get it right.

Note 3 (page 123): Spreadsheets

A spreadsheet is a type of computer program. Spreadsheets look like tables, with rows and columns. The first cell is usually called A1, the one below it is A2, and so on.

	A	B	C	D
1				
2				
3				
4				

In addition to words and numbers, you can type equations into spreadsheet cells. When you do this, the spreadsheet calculates the answers to the equations and displays them.

Equations can refer to values from other cells. For example, you can write an equation that doubles the value typed in the cell above it. To do this, you could type =A1*2 in cell A2 (note that computers often use * instead of × to indicate multiplication). Then, if you type 100 into cell A1, you'd see 200 displayed in cell A2.

The spreadsheet program remembers the equations, so if you change any of the numbers in the spreadsheet, the program will automatically recalculate and display the new answers from the equations.

The most popular spreadsheet program is Microsoft® Excel. Free alternatives you can download include *Apache OpenOffice™* (http://www.openoffice.org/) and *LibreOffice* (https://www.libreoffice.org/). An on-line option is *Google Sheets* (https://docs.google.com/spreadsheet).

Note 4 (page 124): Circular References

Spreadsheet programs (see Note 3) complain about circular references when you type in an equation that tries to use its own result. For example, in cell A1, if you type the equation =A1*2, you'll get a circular reference error. This is because the program would need to know the value of cell A1 before it could calculate the value of cell A1, and that doesn't make sense.

This sort of error can occur if you try to enter an iterative equation (see Note 2) into a spreadsheet. However, there is a way around this (see Note 7).

Note 5 (page 149): Strange Maths

The kind of maths Chandra is talking about is called *calculus*. It's a way of working with equations that describe how the rate of change of something affects something else. For example, we could describe the rabbit population situation (see Note 2) by saying that the rate at which the population increases is proportional to the population.

Sometimes calculus equations can be solved mathematically, giving a new equation that can be used to calculate the answer. Taking the example in Note 2, you can probably see that the population equation is:

$R_y = 100 \times 2^y$

This makes it easy to calculate how many rabbits there'd be in any year, without having to iterate (*ie*, repeat the calculation over and over).

Calculus can be used to study the forest growth problem Jason is looking at. For example, the rate at which trees grow is affected by how much sunlight they get. But as trees grow, they can start to overlap with one another, which reduces the amount of light they get.

Calculus equations can't always be solved mathematically. In such cases, iteration (see Note 2) can be applied to the equations to work out what would happen in the future. Spreadsheets (see Note 3) are one way to do this.

Chandra could see that the problem Jason was working on was a calculus-type problem, and that it needed iteration to solve it. However, because Jason hadn't been taught calculus yet, his spreadsheet was wrong (which is why he was getting circular reference errors— see Note 4). By giving Jason an understanding of the underlying maths, Chandra enabled him to work out how to fix his spreadsheet.

Note 6 (page 150): Mathematical Diagrams

In a complicated system, such as a forest, it can be hard to keep track of what changes what. Diagrams can be very helpful. One good approach is called *system dynamics* (http://en.wikipedia.org/wiki/System_dynamics).

Taking the rabbit population example (see Note 2), we can say that the rabbit population is increased by the rabbit birth rate. Also, the rabbit birth rate is increased by the rabbit population (since the more rabbits there are, the more breeding there'll be). Here is a system dynamics diagram of this:

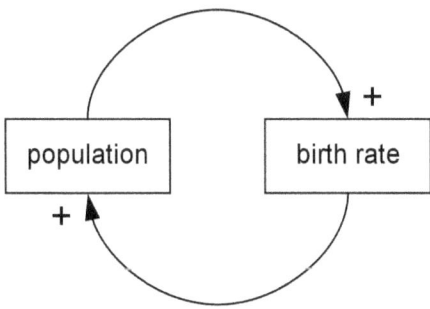

In addition to helping us to understand how a system works, system dynamics diagrams can help to work out what the calculus equations are (see Note 5). System dynamics computer programs can also calculate the behaviour of the system using a similar approach to spreadsheets (see Note 3), and can even draw graphs to illustrate the results.

Note 7 (page 156): No Circular References

Jason had circular references errors (see Note 4) in his spreadsheet because he'd tried to enter an equation that depended on itself (see Note 2). For example, to calculate the rabbit population, he might have entered an equation into cell A1 that said =A1*2. The way to avoid circular references is to modify the equation so that it doesn't depend on itself, but instead it depends on a previously-calculated value. Then, you can copy this equation over and over, so you end up with a list of equations and results like this:

	A	B	C
1	**Equation**	**Result**	**Comment**
2	100	100	Initial number of rabbits
3	=A1*2	200	Number of rabbits after 1 year
4	=A2*2	400	Number of rabbits after 2 years
5	=A3*2	800	Number of rabbits after 3 years
6	=A4*2	1600	Number of rabbits after 4 years
7	=A5*2	3200	Number of rabbits after 5 years

Because it's quick and easy to copy equations, it doesn't take long to create a spreadsheet that can calculate things far into the future.

Note 8 (page 226): Spreadsheet Weirdness

You don't need to understand what's going on with the spreadsheets to follow the story. However, if you want to know, all will be revealed in a later endnote.

Note 9 (page 229): Spreadsheet Weirdness Explained

You don't need to understand what's going on with the spreadsheets to follow the story. However, if you want to know, read on!

Using the network connection he'd set up on Jason's computer, Mr Wherrett was able to see, and change, any of the files on Jason's computer. All the strange results from the spreadsheets were caused by Mr Wherrett changing them without Jason's knowledge.

Jason created two versions of the spreadsheet. The original one, called `Numbers.xls`, was based on the amount of thinning specified in `Numbers.pdf`. The second spreadsheet, `Photo.xls`, was based on the amount of thinning Jason calculated by counting the ribbons on his photos.

Prior to Jason visiting Dr Chandrasekhar on Monday (page 224), Mr Wherrett noticed that Jason had created `Photo.xls`. Because there were a lot of ribbons, this spreadsheet specified a large amount of thinning and showed that that amount of thinning was too much. Obviously Mr Wherrett wouldn't want Jason or anyone else to think this, so to make the result from the new spreadsheet look okay, he changed the amount of thinning back to a smaller value, closer to what `Numbers.pdf` specified.

That evening, Jason discovered the changed value in `Photo.xls` but just assumed he'd made a mistake. He changed it back to what the ribbon count suggested, so the spreadsheet again indicated there was too much thinning.

Later that night, Mr Wherrett noticed that Jason had fixed `Photo.xls`. Jason would have seemed determined to use the large thinning value (from the ribbon photos). Mr Wherrett had to make the two spreadsheets look like they specified about the same amount of thinning; otherwise it would be obvious he was planning to cut down too many trees. Since Jason obviously knew to put the high level of thinning into `Photo.xls`, Mr Wherrett had to put

a   similar   value   into   the   other   spreadsheet
(`Numbers.xls`).

However, putting a large amount of thinning into both spreadsheets would make both of them show that that amount of thinning was excessive. To get around this, Mr Wherrett had to change an equation in both of the spreadsheets. Now, both spreadsheets would incorrectly indicate that a large amount of thinning was okay. It was these spreadsheets that Jason showed Chandra on Tuesday (page 226).

During the meeting with Chandra, Jason noticed that the thinning amount in `Numbers.xls` was too high He put the correct value (from `Numbers.pdf`) back in on Tuesday afternoon. However, because Mr Wherrett had also changed an equation, this spreadsheet now indicated that this amount of thinning was too low.

If you read and understood all that, congratulations!